*Dedicated to the parents, educators,
and all others that make learning fun!*

Copyright © 2020 Ellen Prager

For further information, contact:
Tumblehome, Inc.
201 Newbury St, Suite 201
Boston, MA 02116
http://tumblehomebooks.org/
Library of Congress Control Number 2020951587
ISBN-13 978-1-943431-70-0
ISBN-10 1-943431-70-1

Prager, Ellen
Escape Greenland / Ellen Prager - 1st ed
Illustrated by Tammy Yee

Printed in Taiwan

10 9 8 7 6 5 4 3 2 1

TUMBLEHOME, Inc.

Escape Greenland

Book Two of
The Wonder List Adventures

Ellen Prager

Illustrated by Tammy Yee

DISKO BAY

Ilulissat

Kangia Icefjord

ICE
SHELF

Ilulissat Icefjord
A UNESCO World Heritage Site

The Ice Maze

Beneath Ezzy's feet the ice shifted. The motion wasn't knock-you-off-your-feet big, but enough to get her attention. She'd been about to leap from the giant table-like iceberg she and Luke were on to one that resembled a small castle just a few inches away. Instead, she grabbed hold of her younger brother and froze. Cocking her head, Ezzy listened. At first there were a few deep groans and sonorous cracks, then a thunderous whumpf echoed across the narrow gorge or fjord. "Get down!"

Brother and sister fell to their knees, each of them searching for a nook or crack in the ice to hold onto. They were on the west coast of Greenland, on an iceberg floating in the middle of the Kangia Icefjord. Ancient dark rocks lined the faraway shore and upstream sat the

Jakobshavn (Danish) or Sermeq Kujalleq (Greenlandic) Glacier—the world's fastest flowing river of ice.

It was August and the glacier was rapidly melting. Crystal-clear streams of turquoise blue meltwater rushed across the glacier's surface, cascaded into fractures, and flowed down giant tube-like holes called moulins. At the glacier's front was a humungous, 300-foot-tall, floating cliff or shelf of ice. Here, collapses and calving produced icebergs—tons of icebergs. They drifted downstream through the fjord and out into Disko Bay. The really big bergs eventually reached the open North Atlantic Ocean. But it wasn't a smooth or quick trip into the bay and out to sea—there was an enormous underwater bump in the way.

Most of the fjord was about 1000 feet deep, but at its mouth, where it emptied into Disko Bay, there was an undersea ridge. The ridge caused the depth to decrease abruptly, to just one hundred feet. Icebergs that were too big got stuck on the ridge, which caused a backup or traffic jam of ice in the fjord. Ezzy and Luke were currently stuck in the middle of the ice-choked fjord, huddling together atop an iceberg.

While hiking days earlier, Ezzy had heard a booming noise similar to the one that had just echoed across the fjord. That time, a colossal chunk had broken off the glacier's floating ice shelf and tumbled into the sea. It was the birth of a giant new iceberg. Ezzy had witnessed first-hand what happened next. The collapse at the ice shelf generated a series of waves or a tsunami moving downstream. As the waves traveled through the fjord, the jam-packed icebergs rolled and smashed against one another. Some even tipped completely over.

Knowing what was coming, Ezzy ran her hand across the ice desperate for something to grab onto. She prayed their iceberg wouldn't be of the roll-over variety. Then she found it, a fracture just inches wide. With one gloved hand she gripped the edge of the crack, with the other she reached for her brother. But in trying to find his own handhold, Luke had twisted away from her. Seconds later, all around them the icebergs began to bob up and down, twist and turn. The ice crackled and crunched. A wave was moving through the fjord.

The iceberg they were on suddenly rose and tilted. Luke began to slide. Ezzy reached for him. "Grab my hand!"

Luke tried to grab his sister's hand and their fingers nearly met. But like in a slow-motion disaster movie, inch-by-inch, their hands grew further apart. Luke was sliding away and Ezzy saw what lay behind him. About twenty feet away was a distinct sharp line. It was the edge of the iceberg and a very, very long drop to the sea.

Luke kicked at the ice trying to stop. "Help!"

Thirteen-year-old Ezzy moved quickly. She grasped the fracture's edge with both hands, lay on her stomach, and let her feet slide out toward Luke. "Grab my foot!"

Concentrating, Luke tucked his feet under him and pushed off the ice as best he could, reaching for one of Ezzy's sneakers. His small pudgy hand hit, and he tried to grab hold of her shoe. But Luke couldn't get a good grasp. Then, as his fingers slid off, two tangled in the loops of her shoelace. He quickly grabbed on and slid to a stop. "Phew, that was really close."

Ezzy sighed with relief, until her sneaker started to slip off. "Uh oh."

With her brother hanging on, Ezzy's shoelace had untied. Luke's eyes grew wide. Ezzy carefully tried to pull her foot up toward her chest, hoping she could reach Luke before the sneaker came all the way off.

Another wave rolled through the fjord. Again, the icebergs bumped and twisted, and like a huge frozen bumper car, the one Ezzy and Luke were on rotated and slammed against the adjacent berg. Then it tilted, this time in the opposite direction. Luke slid and crashed into Ezzy. Her sneaker stayed on, but she lost her grip on the ice. Together they began sliding across the iceberg toward its other precipitous edge.

"Hang on," Ezzy urged, hugging her brother.

The iceberg's tilt got steeper and they slid faster. Ezzy kicked at the ice, trying to stop. But to no avail. They kept sliding. She glanced at the iceberg's edge. Beyond was only air and water—deathly cold water very far down. She closed her eyes and hugged Luke even tighter, trying not to think about what it would feel like to plummet into the frigid sea.

No! The new and braver Ezzy wasn't going to give up that easy. She opened her eyes and using one hand tried again to slow their slide, searching for another crack or flaw in the ice, anything to grab onto. But the ice was like a water-slickened Slip 'N Slide and the edge was now only ten feet away.

Just as Ezzy was sure she and Luke were about to plunge to a horrible insta-freeze death, another wave rolled through the fjord. The icebergs bumped and shifted again. Instead of doing a high dive into the cold polar ocean, they slammed hard against a wall—a wall of ice. A taller, steep-sided iceberg had crashed into the one they were on. Ezzy froze, hardly daring to move or even breathe.

Luke didn't hesitate. He wiggled free from his sister's arms, got onto his hands and knees, and then slowly stood. "Phew, that was really *really* close."

That's the understatement of the century, Ezzy thought. She got up carefully. "Looks like the ice has stopped moving, for now. C'mon, let's get out of this crazy frozen maze and find Dad."

Luke nodded. "Which way?"

Ezzy peered across the mile-wide ice-filled fjord. They were about halfway across. She studied the ice, looking for a path through the strange assortment of icebergs jammed tightly between the rock-lined coasts. Melting and calving of the ice had created a lot of weird shapes, like tall skinny mushrooms, arches, and one iceberg that resembled the jagged teeth of a giant. Some icebergs had patches of blue or stripes of brown.

As Ezzy's eyes sought the flattest surfaces possible, she couldn't help but think back a few days and wonder: *How in the world did we get here?*

* * *

Entering the Arctic

Two days earlier.

The airplane was jam packed. Every seat was occupied, and the overhead compartments were so full, Ezzy was sure when they were opened the passengers would all be buried by an avalanche of bags and jackets. She was still surprised by the crowd. Who would have picked Greenland as a vacation hot spot? She'd slept most of the way overnight from Washington, DC to Reykjavik, Iceland and planned to snooze more on this leg of the trip—the three-hour flight to Ilulissat, Greenland.

Sitting between her father in the aisle seat and eleven-year-old Luke at the window, Ezzy dozed—that is until the noise level went from a quiet hush to for-get-about-sleeping loud. All around her, people were now peering out the windows and chatting excitedly. Some of the passengers spoke English, others conversed in languages Ezzy thought she recognized, like Chinese, German, and Spanish. According to her father, the scruffy-looking backpackers sitting in the two rows ahead of them were speaking Danish.

Like so many others in the airplane, Luke had his nose plastered against one of the aircraft's small square windows. "Whoa! Looks like fudge-striped ice cream down there." He turned to his father. "If I had a *phone*, I'd take a photo."

Dr. Skylar passed his phone to the boy. "Use mine. You'll have a phone soon enough. Remember we said when you're twelve or thirteen."

"*But Dad*," Luke said, turning back to the window. "Look at all the cool stuff I could be documenting for school and everything."

Dr. Skylar shook his head and leaned over Ezzy to see out the window. "You're right, it does look fudge stripes down there. That's a glacier. It's like a frozen river transporting ice from Greenland's huge ice sheet to the coast."

Ezzy squeezed in next to her brother. "If it's ice, what are the brown stripes?"

"I read about it," Luke pronounced proudly. "It's dirt scraped off the sides, gets mixed in with the ice."

"Are you sure it's moving?" Ezzy asked. "Doesn't look like it from here."

Dr. Skylar glanced at a page in the guidebook to Greenland he'd been reading. "It says here that some glaciers move very slowly, only about 10 feet per year, but others like the one we're coming to see can move much faster, more than 100 feet in just one day."

"Cool!" Luke said.

Ezzy pretended to shiver. "No, *freezing!*"

"Good one, sis," noted Luke. "They're moving faster because of climate change. Right, Dad?"

"That's right, flowing faster and shrinking." He looked around the plane. "I think that's why so many people are headed to Greenland. To witness the mega-melt first-hand."

"Is that why it was number two on Mom's wonder list?" asked Ezzy.

Her father smiled warmly. "Partly. She was fascinated by icebergs and wanted to come here, to see them first-hand. And of course, the rocks. She was a geologist after all."

"A *marine* geologist," Luke corrected.

Dr. Skylar tussled Luke's hair. "Yup, a marine geologist. Underwater rocks were her specialty, but she also loved animals, just like someone else I know."

"Speaking of animals. Are there *a lot* of wild animals in Greenland?" Ezzy asked, trying to sound unconcerned and nonchalant, as if it was no big deal. She felt better about encountering animals in the wild since their adventure in the Galápagos Islands last summer.

But still she wasn't what you'd call an animal-hugging tree-climbing nature-lover. The unpredictability of wild animals, along with their sharp claws and teeth, still gave her the heebie-jeebies.

Her father showed her some photos in the guidebook. "Hopefully we'll see some seals and whales, maybe a fox or even a reindeer."

"What about polar bears?" Ezzy asked. "They're supposed to be super dangerous and hungry because with all the ice melting there's less food for them."

"I don't think they see them in the part of Greenland we're going to. At least that's what the book says."

"Darn," Luke said.

Ezzy gave him the are-you-serious look, and Luke turned to stare back out the window. "Hey, the fudge stripes are gone. It's just all white down there now."

"We must be over the ice sheet that covers most of Greenland," Dr. Skylar noted.

"It covers more than 600,000 square miles," announced Luke.

In synchrony, Ezzy and her father chuckled and said teasingly, "I read about it!"

Luke pursed his lips and fake scowled at them. "How come it's called Greenland anyway? Looks like it should be called Iceland."

His father nodded. "According to the book, Greenland is mostly ice except near the coast. It says that the man who named it Greenland called it that so people

would want to visit and live there. But maybe Greenland should really be called Iceland, and Iceland Greenland. I hear that Iceland is mostly green except for its
glaciers."

Even though the only thing to see below was an
enormous blanket of white, Luke's attention remained
at the window. Soon a shroud of thick gray clouds ob-
scured what little there was to see.

After another hour or so, the plane dipped lower
and the captain made an announcement. "We've been
cleared for landing. We should have you on the ground
in about fifteen minutes. The temperature's a balmy ten
degrees Celsius or fifty degrees Fahrenheit with light
winds out of the north. Welcome to Greenland."

Ezzy and Luke stayed glued to the window, waiting in suspense to see where they were landing and
what it would look like. But the clouds continued to
mask the landscape below. Then, just before touching
down, the aircraft popped out of the mist. Leaning next
to Luke, Ezzy peered out the window. Low, gray, rocky
hills sped by as they landed, and the airplane raced
down an asphalt runway—a startlingly short runway.
The captain hit the brakes hard, and they were thrown
forward. Luke grabbed Ezzy's hand.

"Hang on to your feet," Dr. Skylar said.

Luke turned to his father. "Hang on to your feet?"

Ezzy chuckled. "I think he meant hang on to your
hat."

As the airplane came to an abrupt stop, Dr. Skylar winked at her. "Hmm, maybe that's it. No matter, we're here."

The airplane taxied back down the runway before making a right turn and heading toward a rectangular red building.

"Is that the airport?" Ezzy asked, thinking it was even smaller than the one in the Galápagos.

"Looks like it," her father replied.

After the airplane stopped, a set of wobbly metal stairs was rolled up to the door. The Skylars, along with the other passengers, disembarked cautiously. The air outside was crisp, cool, and tinged with a slight seaweedy smell. Low-hanging gray clouds continued to mask what lay beyond the runway.

Ezzy zipped up her puffy black jacket. Underneath she had on dark jeans and a long-sleeved black t-shirt with a piece of pizza pictured on the front. On the back it read "The Slice of Life." As usual, her light brown hair was gathered in a ponytail. Around her neck she wore a tattered turquoise scarf with knotted fringe. Lately, Ezzy had been experimenting with clothes. One day she'd go all black and the next match polka dot with stripes. Many of the girls at school tried to dress in the latest fashions, but Ezzy was still trying to figure out her "style" and where she fit in. The one thing she kept the same each day was a scarf.

Ezzy's mother had a drawer full of scarves she'd collected while traveling the world. Ezzy had taken to wearing a different one each week. Some of the kids at school teased her about it, especially when she wore scarves that were a bit ragged or strangely patterned. Her mother had been dead for more than a year now, but Ezzy swore some of the scarves still smelled like her. Ezzy was afraid that as time went on, she would forget all the great things about her mother, even what she looked like. Wearing her mom's scarves made Ezzy feel they were still connected somehow, and it helped keep memories of her mother fresh.

Ezzy glanced around. Based on what she saw— the rocky hills blanketed by clouds, the exceptionally short runway, and the tiny airport—Greenland seemed like a bleak and particularly remote place. She'd had doubts about coming to Greenland. The view, or lack thereof, didn't make her feel more confident in her father's choice for their summer getaway—even if it was number two on her mother's wonder list.

Ezzy lightly slapped her wrist. *Bad Ezzy,* she thought. She'd sworn not to be negative on this trip. She'd had doubts about last summer's trip to the Galápagos too. But after all the craziness on the cruise ship and hijacking, she'd had fun with her brother and father in the islands. She'd also helped to rescue all those people on their ship and save the kidnapped animals.

Last summer's trip had helped Ezzy become more confident and less self-conscious. In school, she'd been less bothered by the clique of "popular" girls that teased her or made a show of ignoring her. Though she still hated getting picked last for teams in gym class. It didn't help that after a recent growth spurt, she was now taller than most of the kids her age.

Ezzy took a deep breath and clenched her fists in determination. She had to stay positive and enjoy the trip for her father and Luke. She reminded herself that this was the new, adventurous Ezzy. She was still uncoordinated, but now she was brave too. Travel to far off, isolated, nowheresville Greenland was something she could do. Besides, it wasn't like last summer, they wouldn't have to deal with sharks, an erupting volcano or some nutjob wildlife smuggler. How bad could it be? What could happen?

*   *   *

Iceberg Capital of the World

After they picked up their roller duffle bags, the Skylars followed the other passengers into the main airport terminal. Ezzy noted that even though the airport was seriously small, it was still bustling with people. Adventurous-looking hikers outfitted with big backpacks and well-worn boots jostled alongside older, more conservative travelers wearing wool jackets and neatly pressed slacks. Nearby, a tightly knit group of Asian tourists followed a young guide holding a sign that read Travel Greenland. Intermixed among the tourists were people who Ezzy figured were the locals. They were generally shorter than the tourists, with darker skin, black hair, and deeply lined, weather-worn faces. A few cute toddlers ran about chased by frenzied adults, presumably their parents.

Ezzy hurried to stay with her dad as he made his way through the crowd. A collection of colorful posters tacked up on the walls drew her attention. Each had a slogan on it typed in big print. One read *Climate Change is Here,* another *See the Melt: Feel the Melt,* along with *Beat the Heat and See the Retreat.*

"Over here. This way, kids," Dr. Skylar shouted, guiding them through an exit.

With their luggage by their sides, the Skylars joined a group of people milling about in the small, otherwise empty parking lot. Within minutes, a mini-bus hauling a flatbed trailer pulled up. Out of the driver's seat popped a young man with a mop of scraggly blonde hair. He wore jeans and a long-sleeved maroon shirt with large lettering down the sleeves. "All those headed to the Arctic Palace, step on up!"

Once the luggage was stowed in the trailer and everyone was aboard the mini-bus, including the Skylars, the wiry young man climbed into the driver's seat. "The name's Anders and it's just a short ride to the hotel."

As the mini-bus lurched forward, Anders shouted, "And . . uh . . you might want to hang on, the road ahead is a little bumpy."

Minutes later, the mini-bus hit a series of rolling, wave-like humps in the road. Ezzy grabbed onto her father, whose head nearly hit the roof with each bump. Luke seized Ezzy's hand as his face began to turn a peculiar shade of green. Based on Anders calling it *just a little bumpy,* Ezzy decided she didn't want to be in a vehicle with the guy if he ever mentioned ditches, holes, or a rough road ahead.

After the organ-shaking, bottom bruising portion of the ride, the road smoothed out. That is until, hardly slowing, Anders sped around a sharp curve. The mini-bus weaved and tilted over. Ezzy could swear the tires on one side lifted clear off the road. Luke's grasp on her hand became a white-knuckle death grip and his coloring went from slightly green to I'm-about-to-blow gray. Ezzy inched away from her brother.

Braking hard, Anders slowed to navigate past a section of road that had collapsed into a ditch. Ezzy ping-ponged her glance between the road and Luke, her commitment to being positive beginning to fade.

After making it around the ditch, the mini-bus sped down a steep hill. Ezzy decided driving around Greenland might be all the adventure they needed.

Low-hanging clouds had continued to obstruct the view of the surrounding landscape. But as they barreled around the next curve, the misty shroud lifted. A series of treeless hills blanketed with small, rectangular, wooden buildings appeared in the distance. The buildings had peaked roofs, and were painted a variety of colors, such as red, light blue, yellow, and olive green. To their right lay a large inlet surrounded by steep cliffs. It was a circular embayment connected to the sea. A series of narrow finger docks lined by small boats sat within the inlet, and tied up along the shore were several larger fishing and cargo ships.

Anders made an abrupt right turn into the parking lot of a long two-story maroon building with white shutters. When the mini-bus came to a stop, Luke released his sister's hand. She shook it out to get the feeling back, while warily inching farther away. His face had turned another worrisome color. It resembled the several-years-old, moldy mac and cheese she'd once found in the back of their refrigerator. Luke was totally fearless around animals, but recently had developed a tendency to get carsick.

"Here we are," announced Anders. "The Arctic Palace Hotel. Go on into reception and I'll bring your bags in."

Ezzy scrambled out of the van. The other passengers appeared happy to be out as well—and still alive. Once inside the hotel, Dr. Skylar waited in line behind the other guests to check in. Ezzy decided to look around.

"Don't go far," her father told her.

With his coloring back to normal human skin tone, Luke followed Ezzy as she skirted a growing pile of luggage. They entered a corridor that led farther into the hotel. On the walls, posters advertised glacier hikes, dog sledding, whale-watching boat trips, and helicopter rides. Luke suddenly sprinted past his sister toward a large floor-to-ceiling window overlooking the coast. "Whoa!"

Ezzy joined him and could hardly believe her eyes. She pulled out her phone to take a photo.

Behind the hotel, the gray, rock-covered, treeless land dipped down to a dark blue-green sea. Thick green moss and scattered tufts of tan grass adorned the rocks. But floating just offshore was the real eye-popper. It was an iceberg—a giant shiny white iceberg bigger than their house at home and wedge-shaped like a ginormous slice of cake.

"Totally awesome!" exclaimed Luke. "Or should I say icesome!"

"Oh no," Ezzy teased. "You're starting to sound like dad."

Just then, their father arrived behind them. "Holy giant iceberg! And this is just the top of the iceberg."

"Tip..." Luke corrected, laughing.

"Don't see that every day!" said an older man joining them and offering to take a photo with the three of them in the picture. He had short snow-white hair, a wide tanned face that wrinkled when he smiled, and an off-white cardigan sweater atop a blue button-down shirt and baggy jeans. "It's hard to tell, but the iceberg is moving with the current."

"Really?" Luke said. "Doesn't look like it."

"Yup, a couple feet an hour." The man leaned down to Luke and pointed to the window frame. "Watch the edge of the iceberg relative to the window frame, a specific point, and you'll be able to see that it's moving."

Luke, Ezzy, and Dr. Skylar stared intently.

A few minutes later Luke turned back to the man. "It *is* moving!"

"Welcome to Ilulissat, the iceberg capital of the world."

Dr. Skylar put out his hand. "I'm Ben Skylar and these are my kids, Ezzy and Luke."

The man shook Dr. Skylar's hand. "So nice to meet you. I'm Hendrik Rise, the owner of the Arctic Palace."

"Nice to meet you, Mr. Rise," Dr. Skylar said.

"Please, call me Hendrik."

Ezzy eyed the man warily. Ever since their experience in the Galápagos, the phrase stranger-danger had taken on a whole new meaning. After all, the guy they'd met and thought was nice last summer had turned out to be an animal-stealing criminal with gun-toting goons who nearly blew them all up.

"How long will you be staying with us?" Hendrik asked.

"We're here for almost a week," Dr. Skylar replied. "My late wife always wanted to come and see your icebergs. She also had colleagues who worked in the area."

"Oh, I'm sorry to hear about your wife. What sort of work did she do?"

Luke raised his chin and puffed out his chest. "She was a marine geologist."

"She was?" Hendrik remarked. "Well, no wonder she wanted to come here. We have a ton of scientists coming through to study our very old rocks and of course, our famous glacier. You know it's the fastest-flowing glacier in the world. And the top producer of icebergs. Did you know that the iceberg that sank the *Titanic* came from our glacier?"

"Really?" said Luke.

"Yes, really." Hendrik turned to Dr. Skylar. "Are you a scientist as well?

"No, no. I'm a surgeon."

"That could come in handy here as well. These days we have more scientists around than doctors and the ice sheet and glacier are dangerous places to work. Deep crevasses and collapses, especially now."

"You mean because of climate change?" Ezzy asked. "Is that why so many people are here?"

"Yes. We call them clima-tourists. They're here to see the ice melting up close and personal. Though it's a bit of a mystery, really, why the glacier here is melting so much faster than other glaciers and exactly how it's happening. I'm supporting a team of researchers who are trying to figure out what's going on. If you'd like, I can introduce you later... or maybe right now." He waved at a couple passing through the corridor behind them.

The man and woman waved back and approached the group. Each wore a faded orange puffy vest over a long-sleeved shirt with jeans. The woman was slim, had intense blue eyes, wavy shoulder-length auburn hair, and appeared to be about Dr. Skylar's age. The man was younger and African American. He wore his black hair in a man-bun atop his head and had a rugged, easy-going look about him.

"This is Drs. Dixon and Johnson," said Hendrik. "They are part of the team working on the glacier. And this is the Skylar family."

"Skylar?" asked the woman. "You're not related to Dr. Evelyn Skylar are you?"

"Indeed we are, she was my wife."

"Well, what do you know. I'm Maggie and I went to graduate school with Evelyn. I was so sorry to hear of her passing. It is a true loss for all of us." She then turned to Luke and Ezzy. "Your mother was a real pistol, always first to volunteer or jump in. We learned how to rappel together."

"Really?" Luke said again, while Ezzy fingered the scarf she was wearing.

"Really," Maggie replied. "You must be Luke, and there's no mistaking you, young lady. You must be Ezmeralda or should I say Ezzy?"

Ezzy blushed at the use of her full name, wondering why her parents couldn't have chosen something normal like Sara or Robin.

"It's so nice to meet you," Dr. Skylar said. "We'd love to hear about your work."

Hendrik nodded to the group. "Well, glad you all could meet. If there's anything else you need, please let me know."

"Thanks again," said the man, Dr. Johnson. "We're heading out first thing in the morning and will let you know how it goes."

As Hendrik left, the two scientists explained how they'd flown in two weeks earlier and were part of a team studying the nearby glacier. They were documenting how fast it was melting and trying to figure out how and why the ice was disappearing so rapidly.

"Tomorrow, crazy Maggie here," Dr. Johnson told them, "is going to rappel into one of the glacier's giant holes, or moulins as we call them, to do some mapping and deploy a camera and GPS sensor."

Luke's eyes grew wide.

"Yup!" Maggie agreed.

"Isn't that kinda *dangerous*?" Ezzy asked.

The scientist smiled and shrugged as if it was nothing. "Done it plenty of times. It's all in the planning and preparation. Safety first. We've been scouting the site for days now and know where it is safe and where it isn't. We'll reconnoiter the area once more, just to be sure before going in, and of course, we'll check our equipment again."

"Just a drop in the old pail," Dr. Skylar said to his kids.

Luke laughed. "Bucket, dad."

Ezzy rolled her eyes.

"Thing is we really need to know what's going

on in and under the glacier, not just on the surface," Dr. Johnson added. "It's actually quite amazing. We've discovered that some of the big moulins connect under the ice. We think the meltwater rushing down has created a network of under-the-ice tunnels or rivers. We're going to try to explore and map them."

"Awesome," said Luke.

"Yes, that is amazing," said Dr. Skylar.

Or completely crazy, thought Ezzy.

"It's very exciting," Maggie added. "But it's slow going working on the ice. Typical field work issues like equipment breaking down and such. But if everything goes well, we should be back in a few days. Maybe we can get together then and go for a hike."

"That would be great," replied Dr. Skylar. "Right, kids?"

Ezzy and Luke nodded.

The scientists left, and the Skylar family headed to their room to unpack and get settled in. They had reserved a small suite with two bedrooms and bathrooms and a little family-style living room in the middle outfitted with a couch, two chairs, a coffee table, and a flat screen television. It was comfortable, but nothing fancy.

Luke immediately turned on the television. All that came up was static. Ezzy thought, yup, nowheresville. Luke shrugged and turned it off. He and Ezzy checked out the bedrooms.

"You two get the one with two beds," their father announced. "Let's unpack and get ready for dinner."

Ezzy's stomach growled. She suddenly realized how hungry she was. She looked out the window and noticed it was still light outside, like early afternoon. "What time is it anyway?"

Dr. Skylar glanced at his watch, which he had adjusted on the plane to the correct time. "Six PM. Remember, this time of year here the sun never sets. But in winter, it's dark 24/7."

From his suitcase, Luke whipped out one of the dark eye masks his father had given him and Ezzy for sleeping. "I'm ready, Dad. But I also kinda want to get up to see what it looks like at midnight with the sun still up."

"Me too," his father said. "I can set an alarm and we can all get up."

Ezzy looked at the two of them, shaking her head. "No thanks, I highly value my sleeping time."

"C'mon sis," Luke urged.

"Nope. You two are all on your own when it comes to late night strolls through the wilderness."

Luke rolled his eyes at his sister before turning to his father. "What are we doing tomorrow? Are we going to see more icebergs?"

Before he could answer, a loud and eerie howl sounded from outside the hotel. Ezzy froze. Were there wolves in Greenland? Then, as if in response, there was another, this time longer and more piercing howl. Soon it was a symphony of scary, eerie howling. *Were there a whole lot of wolves in Greenland? Wolves definitely fell into the category of wild animals with sharp claws and large teeth.* Some sounded very close. "Uh, what's going on?"

Her father went to the window. "Can't see anything from here. Sounds like it's coming from out back. Let's go check it out." He headed for the door.

Ezzy stayed put. "Seriously? I think I'll wait here."

Luke grabbed her hand. "C'mon sis, you gotta come!"

As the strange howling continued, Ezzy was basically dragged out the door by her younger, but surprisingly strong brother.

*   *   *

Daylight, Dogs, and Dinner

Being on the menu for a pack of wolves was definitely not on Ezzy's to-do list in Greenland or anywhere else. She lagged behind her father and brother as they dashed down the corridor to a doorway that led outside and behind the Arctic Palace.

"Hang on, Luke!" Dr. Skylar called to his son, who had scampered ahead. "Wait up."

Ezzy followed, warily stepping outside onto a small wood porch. Luke had already run down the stairs to the rocks below. At first it was quiet, but then from somewhere faraway came a deep and bone-chilling howl. In response, a cacophony of cries arose both distant and near. Ezzy looked to the rock-covered area behind the hotel. Scattered among the gray rocks and mounds of tall grass were what looked very much like large tan wolves. With thick fur, small peaked ears, and a slightly pointed snout, each of the animals sat on well-muscled haunches, howling skyward. The sound was like nothing Ezzy had heard, a doleful yet eerie pleading—as if the creatures longed for something un-obtainable. She hoped it wasn't fresh meat in the form of new hotel guests.

An older, stocky man carrying a bucket strode into view. A girl about Luke's age trailed behind. The man wore dirty jeans tucked into black knee-high rubber boots, a worn T-shirt, and a baseball cap. The scowl on his dark ruddy-skinned face matched his gruff tone as he called out. "Okay, you fur balls, enough of that already."

Walking with a slight limp, the man reached into the bucket. He pulled out remarkably large hunks of fish and tossed them to the animals. The wolves, if that's what they were, began chomping on the big chunks-o-fish.

The young girl also wore boots and jeans, along with a lightweight pink sweater. As she skipped along behind the man, her short dark pigtails bounced in a perky rhythm. The girl glanced toward the hotel and put up a hand as if to wave, but then got distracted by something to their right. Ezzy turned just in time to see a blur of scurrying fur race toward her brother.

Ezzy and Dr. Skylar sprinted to the boy as he was knocked to the ground. By the time they reached him, Luke lay flat on his back, giggling. Climbing all over him and using his face as a human lollipop were three furry puppies.

The young girl ran over. "Kali, Dante, Donner, stop that. Come here."

Two of the pups stopped joyfully mauling Luke and scurried over to the girl. "Sit," she said. The pups stared at her. "Sit!"

Meanwhile, the third puppy had grabbed the toe of Luke's sneaker. Shaking its head, the puppy pulled and growled playfully. Luke laughed and pulled back.

"Stop it, Dante!" ordered the girl. "Come!"

The puppy released Luke's sneaker and ran to the girl. Dr. Skylar helped Luke up. A seagull landed nearby. When it began to squawk, the three puppies took off to chase it.

The girl rolled her eyes. "Come!" she shouted. "Come here!"

Once they'd scared the seagull off, the pups scampered back to the girl. She shrugged and turned to the Skylars. "Trying to break them of that, chasing birds. But they're just puppies."

"Are they wolves?" Ezzy asked.

"No," replied the girl, brushing back several strands of hair that had fallen into her cute, slightly-pug-nosed-face. "They're Greenland dogs. Sled dogs. The best pullers ever and the only kind of dogs here in Greenland."

Luke looked surprised. "Really? How come?"

The girl's face lit up and she stood a little straighter. "The dogs are part of our history and culture. It's how we get around on the ice and hunt. If we let other dogs mix with them, we could lose the breed." A little softer and nodding toward the man still feeding the dogs, she added, "That's what my dad told me."

"What's with all the weird howling?" Ezzy inquired.

The girl laughed. "Everyone always asks that. Happens every day at about the same time. Partly it's when we feed them and because it's just the way they are. Once one dog starts, they all get going."

Luke pointed to a dog nearby. It was tied to a length of chain about fifteen feet long. "How come they're tied up like that?"

"It's for their own good. So they don't get into any trouble. They don't mind. Summer is mostly when they rest. In the winter we keep them really busy." She paused. "Well, at least we used to."

"What do you mean?" questioned Dr. Skylar.

"There isn't as much ice around anymore and it isn't very thick. A couple of dogs fell through last winter. It's getting dangerous."

Before she could say anything else, her father approached the group. "Come along Katya, and leave these people be."

Katya waved as she walked away, trailed by the puppies.

The Skylars waved back. After a quick stop in their room to wash up, the family headed to the hotel restaurant for dinner. Thinking of her growling stomach and dinner, and how remote the place was, Ezzy couldn't help but wonder what would be on the menu. She remembered that there were reindeer in Greenland. Ezzy hoped they weren't considered fine dining, as that would be like eating Santa's sleigh team.

*   *   *

Ezzy and Luke stared at the dinner menu.

Luke shook his head. "Nope. Not going to happen. No way am I eating that." He turned to his father. "People don't really order it, do they?"

Ezzy stuck out her tongue. "Yuck! Not me."

"Agreed," their father replied. "But the people here have a long history of eating seal and whale meat. It's part of their culture."

"What about musk ox burger?" Ezzy asked. "What the heck is a musk ox anyway?"

"I think it's kind of like a buffalo," Dr. Skylar answered.

Luke frowned. "But there's plenty of other stuff to eat now. Why still eat seals and whales?"

"It's the conditions here, son, they're very harsh. It's hard to grow or raise things, so a lot of stuff has to be imported and that makes it very expensive. It's easy to judge people based on how we live. Don't get me wrong, I don't support killing seals or whales for meat, but I do understand why they do it."

Luke shook his head again. "Yeah, well I'm still not going to eat it!"

"Yeah, me either," added Ezzy. "Bleck!"

"You know there's a big push to eat less meat altogether because it's better for the planet," Dr. Skylar told them.

Luke scrunched up his round, freckled face. Ezzy snickered. It was the look he got whenever he was thinking hard about something. But she also thought it was how he looked when he had to go to the bathroom—really bad.

"Hey, maybe they can serve that Impossible Burger!" Luke suggested. "Remember we tried one and it was pretty good? I've even been thinking about giving up regular hamburgers."

Ezzy stared wide-eyed at her brother. "Really? But I thought that was like your favorite food ever, after French fries, that is."

Luke's chin rose as he announced in a very serious adult-like tone, "Sometimes we have to change our behavior to do what is right. Besides, cows are pretty cute, and I read that they're actually smart too."

Ezzy stared at the menu. "Not many choices then. How do you feel about fish?"

Luke shrugged. "I'm trying to eat sustainable species."

Dr. Skylar tussled Luke's hair. "You are an example for all of us, son. How about you Ez, what's on your menu these days?"

"Working on it, Dad. I swear I'm trying to eat more veggies and stuff, but not sure I'm ready to give up on real burgers yet."

Her father smiled. "Right there with you, kid. We'll work on it together."

The waitress came by to take their order. Luke and Ezzy ordered fish and chips, while Dr. Skylar went with a more adventurous choice—musk ox burger. Meanwhile, outside the wall of windows that over-looked the coast, the giant piece-o-cake iceberg they'd spied earlier had floated further downstream. Behind it, a few smaller chunks of ice drifted northward.

Following a bite of his musk ox burger, Dr. Skylar gave a thumbs up. "Not bad." He then pulled out a pa-per he had tucked into his pocket. It was a map of hik-ing trails along the shoreline of the Kangia Icefjord. "So tomorrow I thought we'd go out for a short hike to see the icefjord and more icebergs, and then the following day we have a choice of kayaking or a boat ride north to see another glacier."

"Kayaking?" Ezzy responded. "You must be joking. The water here is like a bajillion degrees cold."

Dr. Skylar laughed. "That's why we brought long underwear and they give you a dry suit."

"A dry suit?" asked Luke.

"Like a wetsuit, except it keeps the water out so you stay totally dry even if you fall in."

Ezzy stared at her father skeptically. "I definitely vote for option two and no insta-freeze falling in."

Just then Hendrik, the owner of the hotel, approached their table. Alongside him was a thin woman wearing an elegant matching beige cashmere sweater and dress combination. Long strands of sparkly diamonds hung from her ears. Cut in a shining blunt bob, her white-blond hair was perfectly coiffed. Ezzy unconsciously smoothed the fly-away hairs from her ponytail and glanced down at her black jeans and pizza-slice t-shirt. She suddenly felt exceptionally underdressed.

"Hello Skylar family," said Hendrik. "How's dinner?"

"Excellent, thank you," replied Dr. Skylar.

"I'd like you to meet my wife, Sarina Louise."

"Oh Hendrik, please. Everyone just calls me SL," said the woman. "It's lovely to meet you." She moved closer and smiled demurely.

Ezzy leaned back and tried not to make a face or cough. When she saw Luke scrunch up his nose and look like he'd just tasted something especially vile, she almost burst out laughing. It was the woman's perfume. As soon as she got close, the smell was overwhelming. Ezzy didn't know exactly how to describe it, odor-de-stinky, like a cross between moth balls and a cloying chemical sweetness. Ezzy's nose began to tickle. She knew what was coming and couldn't stop it. Covering her face, she sneezed.

"Bless you," said SL.

"Would you like to join us for dessert?" Dr. Skylar asked.

Noooo, thought Ezzy, *not that, it'll be an international incident. They'll have to call 9-1-1 when a family suffocates due to a cloud of super-stink perfume.*

"Oh, no thank you," Hendrik replied. "We've got a dinner meeting with some potential investors. We're expanding... hopefully." He winked and turned to wave to a small group outfitted in business suits that had just arrived at the restaurant. Before leaving, he added, "I recommend the flourless chocolate cake."

After they'd gone, Ezzy breathed (but not too deeply) a sigh of relief. Given where they were, she thought it only appropriate to order *ice* cream for dessert, while her father and Luke tried the chocolate cake. They then headed to their room. Once inside, Ezzy glanced out the window. It was still light out, yet she was exhausted. Then she remembered that even though it wasn't dark, it was probably pretty late.

After so many hours of travel, the entire family quickly fell asleep. Dr. Skylar was so tired he forgot to set his alarm so he and Luke could get up to see Greenland's famous midnight sun. But at about that time, just outside the back door of the hotel, one person was awake and walking by as quietly as possible.

He was outfitted with a backpack and for all appearances was a tourist going on a late-night hike to enjoy Greenland's twenty-four-hour sun. But if someone looked more closely, he or she would have noticed that the apparent backpacker carried a rifle and had a large wrench strapped to the bottom of his pack. Silently, he made his way unnoticed toward the Kangia Icefjord.

*   *   *

The Icefjord

When Dr. Skylar attempted to rouse his kids the next morning, it was like trying to wrestle two bears from hibernation mid-winter.

"C'mon, you sleepy heads," he prodded. "Up, up, up, we want to beat the crowds out on the hike."

Through half-closed eyes and a sleep-fuzzed brain, Ezzy groaned, "Crowds? Dad, it's Greenland. It's not like we're at Disney World on spring break. I think we'll be okay."

"You snooze, you won't get there first," he replied.

A muffled chuckle arose from Luke's pillow. "Lose, Dad. You snooze, you lose. That's how it goes."

"That's right. Now let's get a move on. I've laid out your hiking clothes and shoes. We'll have a quick breakfast to fuel up and then be off on the hunt for more icebergs."

At the mention of icebergs, Luke sat up, stretched and jumped from his bed onto Ezzy's, and shook her playfully. "C'mon Ezmeralda," he teased.

"Ugh," she moaned, burying her head under the pillow.

After enough poking from Luke and encouragement from her father, Ezzy got up. She and Luke dressed, and the family headed to breakfast. Luke and his father went directly to the buffet. Meanwhile, Ezzy found a table, sat, and laid her head down, closing her eyes. Maybe she could sneak in a few more minutes of sleep.

"Got ya a muffin and some eggs," her father said as he rubbed Ezzy's back and put a plate down in front of her.

"Mmmm, thanks," she muttered.

"Wake up, Ez," Luke urged. "There's a new cool-looking iceberg out there."

Ezzy raised her head and opened one eye. Then she sat up to see better. Sure enough, another large iceberg was floating by offshore. It was the strangest looking iceberg Ezzy had ever seen, not that she'd seen very many. But even in photos she'd never seen anything like this one. It was a fantastical Dr. Seuss iceberg. Overall it was the size of a building and had a sort of triangular shape with a peaked top. At its base were two rounded corners separated by a large arch over the water. The arch was big enough for a boat to cruise right underneath. Its rounded corners appeared as if they'd been sculpted into stacks of flying saucers. Added to all that was a slight turquoise tinge. "Whoa."

A strong smell drew Ezzy's attention. She wrinkled her nose and wondered if Hendrik's wife SL was nearby. She looked around and didn't see the woman. "What is that smell?"

Luke laughed, pinched his nose, and pointed to his father's plate.

"I'm trying some of the local breakfast delicacies. Pickled fish and this rather strong smelling cheese."

"Ugh!" Ezzy groaned and moved over a seat.

"Oh c'mon," her father said. "It's not that bad."

Luke got up and moved next to his sister, nodding to his father.

After breakfast, they stopped by their room to retrieve their backpacks and water bottles. Following the map Dr. Skylar had picked up the day before, they walked through the hotel parking lot and crossed the road to a wooden staircase. While climbing the stairs, Ezzy couldn't help but notice the rocks in the underlying cliff. They were pinkish with wavy black stripes.

Dr. Skylar stopped to take a photo. "Your mom would have loved these rocks."

"Yeah, she probably would have whipped out that rock hammer she always carried," Ezzy added, chuckling. "and started chipping off pieces to take home."

"Right you are, Ez. Our luggage was always so much heavier on the way home. Like that time when your mom and I went to the Bahamas. On the way home the customs agent picked up my bag and said, "Sir, what do you have in here? Rocks?"

Luke laughed. "And you said, *Exactly*. Dad, you always tell that story."

"Exactly," Dr. Skylar repeated.

A boardwalk extended from the top of the stairs south. In the distance, a dark ridge lined the horizon. Off to their right was a small parking lot and to the left was a building under construction.

Dr. Skylar led them to a large sign adjacent to the boardwalk. He stepped closer and read, "East Entrance Kangia Icefjord Trails. Hikers should be well prepared before starting out. There are no facilities or services out on the trails and your communication devices probably won't work. Be sure to wear appropriate clothing, adequate footwear, and bring plenty of water, insect repellent, and food as needed."

Yup, middle of nowhere, Ezzy thought again.

Luke stepped up to the sign, pointing to smaller text printed below. "Hey, look there's more." He leaned in closer to read. "Also watch out for the unusually large Greenland mosquitoes around dusk, hidden holes in the ground due to permafrost thaw, and do not pet or get close to stray dogs, reindeers, musk ox or wild foxes. Going off the trails is not recommended, and swimming is prohibited."

"Swimming?" Luke questioned.

"Unusually large mosquitoes and wild foxes?" Ezzy added. "Are you sure about this Dad?"

"Oh, they probably have to put that there for liability issues. The guidebooks all say it's perfectly safe."

Luke and Ezzy glanced at one another and then back at their father.

"C'mon, it'll be an adventure."

Ezzy hoped it wasn't like their lives-were-at-risk adventure last summer. She had traded in her clothing of choice for what her father insisted they wear—thick khaki hiking pants, a long-sleeved sweat-wicking shirt, a fleece vest, topped by a windbreaker. She had, however, added one more thing to the outfit—another of her mother's scarves. This one was light purple, fuzzy, and super soft. Looking around she noted, "Well, we definitely beat the crowd, Dad."

There was no one else in sight.

"You know what they say. Early bird catches the fun."

Ezzy and Luke stared at their father.

Luke laughed. "Worm, Dad. Worm. Early bird catches the worm."

Dr. Skylar smiled. "Yeah, that too."

"But really," Luke said. "If this place is so popular, where is everyone?"

"They're probably still sleeping like normal people," Ezzy announced only half-jokingly.

"Oh, you two," their father teased. "This is the best time of the day, and besides, it will be so much better without a lot of people around. The true wilderness."

"So much better," Ezzy moaned.

Ezzy and Luke followed their father as he set out along the boardwalk, which wound around rocks and over large tufts of grass. It was sunny with a cool breeze and just a few clouds overhead.

Luke pointed to some mud and a small depression filled with water beneath the boardwalk. "Is that why they built this?"

"Could be," Dr. Skylar answered.

Off to the side, among a scattering of miniature houses, sat several sled dogs. One lay resting, while the others watched the group with pricked-up ears and curious eyes. After about fifteen minutes of easy walking, the boardwalk ended. A pile of wooden boards lay near the end of the walkway.

Luke stepped up to read a sign nearby. "Under construction. Donated by Hendrik and Sarina Louise Rise."

Dr. Skylar glanced at the trail map. "C'mon. I think the icefjord is just over the ridge up ahead."

A narrow packed-dirt trail led around a small pond to a hill of smooth, gray, gradually sloping rocks. Strange orange and black crinkly patches grew atop the rocks, and in between were thick, mossy-looking gray plants. It was the base of the ridge they'd seen in the distance. Dots of blue paint on the rocks marked the trail. After they climbed for a bit, Ezzy stopped to take off her jacket, which she put in her backpack.

"I think we should be able to see the fjord from the top," Dr. Skylar noted.

Nearing the ridge's peak, Luke scrambled ahead. At the top, he stopped abruptly. "Wicked!"

Dr. Skylar joined him. "Wowza!"

Ezzy made it up as well and stood, mouth agape. She didn't even have a snarky remark to make. The view was simply too astonishing.

Icebergs. Lots of icebergs. Big ones, little ones, square-shaped ones, pointy ones. Some of the icebergs resembled familiar shapes like a ski slope or a blocky mountain top, whereas others were more of the abstract melted art variety. It was a smorgasbord of icebergs all jammed together floating between the rock-lined coasts of the V-shaped fjord. Until that very moment, Ezzy hadn't really known what an icefjord was. Now she got it—a narrow, rocky valley filled with ocean topped by icebergs. She pulled out her phone and snapped a few photos.

"Now, if I had a phone, I could take photos too," Luke observed.

"This is a memory to last a lifetime, with or without a camera," Dr. Skylar told his son. "I want you both to live in the moment while we're here, not spend all your time taking photos." He then reached into his pocket, pulled out his phone, and handed it to Luke.

"But then again, how often do you see this!"

Thick, puffy, gray clouds hung over the icefjord. Suddenly, a hole opened in the clouds, and a beam of sunlight shone through, striking a three-peaked mountainous iceberg smack in the middle of the fjord. Its white ice gleamed brighter than everything around it, as if highlighted by a Hollywood spotlight.

Dr. Skylar removed his good camera from his backpack and took several photos. "Okay, even I can't resist taking a photo of that. Your mother was right, as usual. This is incredible."

Eyes wide, Luke nodded vigorously. "Can we go closer?"

"Sure, looks like that's where the trail heads," his father replied before leading them off the ridge toward the icefjord. Still taking in the mind-blowing, couldn't-have-imagined, ice-filled view, Ezzy nearly tripped as she headed down the rocks. Typical, she thought. A little braver—maybe. Coordinated—still no.

They came to an intersection and stood again looking at the icefjord. The clouds had shifted, and now half the icebergs gleamed in the sunlight. Everywhere she looked, Ezzy saw something new in the ice. An opening in one iceberg was like the entrance to a shadowy cave. On another was a kiddy-pool-sized depression filled with crystal clear turquoise water.

"Let's go left here," Dr. Skylar suggested. "To the next ridge upstream to see more of the fjord."

They hiked along the coast further up the fjord.

Soon the trail over the rocks widened and became packed dirt, littered with loose tan pebbles. Luke again raced ahead and up a short steep hill. At the top, he stopped, and the others joined him to take in another breathtaking view. It was another section of the icefjord and a whole new collection of wondrous and weirdly shaped icebergs.

Luke pointed to a side trail that descended to a small rock-strewn beach "Can we go down there, Dad?"

"I don't see why not. But be careful. Don't want any falls out here."

No joke, Ezzy thought. Thinking about what would happen if one of them fell, she pulled out her phone to check for a signal. Nope.

Luke scrambled down the trail to a rock ledge a little more than a foot high. Ezzy made her way down more carefully, followed by her father. After they had jumped down onto the rock-covered beach, Luke led them across the rounded stones to the water's edge. The water was calm, clear, and only a few inches deep. Ezzy tentatively reached down. Freezing, just as she'd expected.

Luke pointed to a car-sized iceberg floating about twenty feet away. "Whoa! That one looks like it's bleeding."

"Yeah, brown blood," Ezzy added. "Kinda creepy."

"It's the sediment in the ice," their father said. "It must be flowing out with the water as the ice melts."

"Awesome!" Luke exclaimed.

Ezzy turned to examine an iceberg off to their right. It too was about twenty feet away, separated from the beach by an area of open water. It was shaped like a mound topped by a cluster of three odd looking structures that had formed as the ice melted. "That one looks like a clump of tall skinny mushrooms."

Luke pointed to another iceberg. "That one looks like a cyclops alligator with a big blue spot for an eye."

"You're right, it does," said his father. "You know, I was reading about the colors of the ice on the plane. The white ice has air in it. The brown ice has dirt in it. And because it's darker than the white ice, it absorbs the sun's heat faster and melts quicker than the lighter colored ice."

Luke nodded. "What about the blue ice?"

"That's ice without air in it."

Scrunching up his face in thought, Luke asked, "Like if there was a lot of ice on top of it, the air would be squeezed out by the weight?"

"Exactly," his father answered.

Little ripples in the water drew Ezzy's attention downward. She stepped back, wondering what had caused the small waves. Then, no more than a foot away, a small whiskered silvery face popped up. Startled, Ezzy jumped back and tripped, falling onto her butt.

Luke giggled. "It's a seal, sis."

"Ouch," muttered Ezzy, rubbing her backside as her heart raced. "Yeah, I can see that now."

Her father reached out a hand to help her up. "Okay?"

Ezzy nodded. Physically she was fine, it was just a little fall. But it was still embarrassing. She chalked it up as another incident of the uncoordinated.

The silvery-gray, blubbery, spotted seal lay in the shallow water. It had big dark eyes and a cute little whiskered snout. The seal stared curiously at Luke. He took a step closer.

"Not too close," his father urged. "Don't want to scare it."

Ezzy's pulse slowed as she recovered from her seal surprise. Then, a deep, thunderous rumble echoed across the fjord. She jerked her head around. "What was that?"

They all looked about, searching for the source of the booming noise. When Ezzy turned back to look at the seal, it was gone.

"What was that?" Luke repeated to his father.

Their father had the same look on his face that Luke got when he was deep in thought.

Moments later the icebergs in the fjord began to rock back and forth. Cracks, groans, and splashes resounded. The water at their feet sloshed and a bigger wave rolled toward the beach. Ezzy and Luke moved back to avoid getting wet.

Dr. Skylar's brow creased as he turned upstream. "Kids, let's go back to the trail."

"Why?" Luke asked. "What—"

Before he could finish, the icebergs began to jostle and rock more violently. They slammed against one another, and the sounds of crashing and cracking rang out. Nearby, a pyramid-shaped iceberg flipped upside down. On its underside was a patchwork of blue and dark brown ice.

"Hustle up," Dr Skylar urged, making his way back across the stone-covered beach. Ezzy and Luke followed.

In the fjord, the icebergs continued to roll, bob up and down, and bang against one another. The mushroom iceberg split apart and three ice-shrooms crashed into the water. Another, even bigger, iceberg broke apart, generating a much larger wave. It rolled toward shore. Luke and Ezzy were still crossing the rocks when the wave struck. A cold spray hit Ezzy as a surge of frigid water raced toward them across the rocky beach.

Luke reached the ledge and his father pulled him up onto it. Ezzy readied to leap up to join them, when the rock she was on wobbled. Water rushed toward her. Ezzy began to fall. Before she could do a full face plant and get a literally ice-cold bath, a strong hand gripped her arm. Her father had leapt down and grabbed her. He pushed Ezzy onto the ledge and jumped up just as the frigid seawater surged below across the beach.

"What's going on?" Luke asked.

Dr. Skylar paused. "Do you remember watching that movie *Chasing Ice?*"

Luke nodded.

"Do you remember the part when a huge section of the glacier and ice shelf collapsed?"

"Yeah."

"That part of the movie was actually filmed upstream of here. I bet another big piece broke off. Not as big as in the movie, but enough to create waves moving through the fjord."

"Is that what that loud noise was?" Ezzy asked.

"I think so."

Ezzy shook her head. "Yeah, well they should have said something about that on those warning signs."

"You're right," her father replied.

He suggested they take a short rest so they sat on some flat-topped rocks. From his backpack, Dr. Skylar passed out a mix of nuts, fruit, and chocolate. The icebergs soon quieted. But then, from higher up in the fjord, came a new sound. It was rhythmic and thumping.

*   *   *

Mishap at the Moulin

Ezzy and Luke stood, turning upstream. The rhythmic thumping sound was coming from that direction and getting louder.

"What's that?" Luke asked.

Just then, a large red shape emerged from behind the next ridge upstream. It was a helicopter flying low along the shoreline, headed in their direction. As the Skylars watched, it came closer and began to slow. Once overhead, wind from the helicopter's rotating blades whirled sand around them and kicked up dust. Shielding their eyes, they huddled together.

The helicopter hovered for a moment before slowly flying to the north and disappearing behind another rocky ridge. The thumping sound of its beating blades died away surprisingly fast.

"*Who* was that?" Ezzy asked.

"No idea," her father replied.

Minutes later, two men in red jumpsuits appeared, jogging over the ridge and waving at the Skylars. Dr. Skylar grabbed his backpack and headed toward them. "C'mon kids."

Ezzy and Luke slung their smaller packs over their shoulders and followed.

As Ezzy got closer, she noticed the expression on the men's faces. Something bad had happened. When Ezzy got near enough to hear, one man was speaking to her father and gesturing toward the helicopter. "There's a rescue team already climbing down. We heard you were a doctor. When we contacted the hotel, someone said they'd seen you heading for the hiking trails."

"How bad is it? What can I do to help?" Dr. Skylar asked.

"Could you come with us up to the glacier front? It's a short ride. Otherwise it might be a while until a doctor can be found and get on site. It's unclear how bad the injuries are."

"Sure, but I only have a first aid kit in my pack, and what about my kids?" He turned to Luke and Ezzy.

"We've got medical supplies with us, and they have some at the camp. The kids can come, and once we drop you off, we can take them back to the hotel either before or after transporting the victim out."

Dr. Skylar agreed, and the family followed the men

to the waiting helicopter. Along the way, Ezzy tapped her dad on the back. "What happened?"

"There was an accident up on the glacier."

At the rescue helicopter, one of the men helped Ezzy climb into the rear passenger compartment. But Luke hung back, shaking his head.

"You're next, Luke," his father encouraged.

"Can we hike back instead?"

"Son, what's wrong?"

Ezzy thought about how Luke was typically so adventurous, ready and able to go with the flow. It was something Ezzy admired about her brother and sometimes was even jealous of. She often felt like he'd been the sole heir to their mother's adventure gene. Then she remembered how green Luke had looked in the mini-bus. *He must be afraid of getting motion sick,* she thought. Ezzy almost teased her brother, but then thought better of it. "C'mon Luke. You can sit next to me. I could use your help, buddy. It looks kinda scary."

Luke gazed up at Ezzy and his frown lessened. He let the men and his father help him into the helicopter. As he was being strapped in, Ezzy grabbed hold of Luke's hand as if she needed to hold on for reassurance.

Lifting off, the aircraft lurched sideways, buffeted by wind. Luke shut his eyes as Ezzy tightened her grip on his hand.

They flew upstream along the rocky shore of the

fjord. Ezzy craned her neck to get a view out the side windows. Below, the traffic jam of ice had begun to thin, and Ezzy was surprised to see an area of open water. Then, an enormous vertical cliff of ice appeared. It was hundreds of feet tall. They flew on. The ice below again changed, becoming bluish and deeply fractured. There were scattered patches and stripes of brown. It resembled an otherworldly landscape of giant, frozen, blue-hued pinnacles.

The helicopter dropped abruptly, and one of the men shouted to the kids, "A little turbulence. Nothing to worry about."

Ezzy's stomach had dropped as well, and Luke had turned a new and distressing shade of green. The helicopter slowed and soon began to hover. It then gradually lowered until Ezzy felt a bump and heard the rotating blades slow. They had landed.

Luke took a deep breath as a normal skin tone returned to his face. One of the men inside slid open the side door. "We got a call from the rescue team. The victim is being stabilized and will be pulled up soon. It's about a fifteen to twenty-minute hike to camp and then a short way from there. They'd like you, Dr. Skylar, to come as quickly as possible."

"What about my kids?"

"We can take them back and return before you're ready to transport. And we'll call ahead to the hotel to let them know we're coming so someone can meet the helicopter. I'm sure they'll be happy to watch over your family while you help out."

Dr. Skylar turned to Ezzy and Luke. "Is that okay with you two?"

"Of course, Dad," Ezzy answered. "We'll be fine. Go help."

"Yeah, Dad," added Luke, looking a little woozy. "Go help."

Dr. Skylar hugged his children, grabbed his backpack, and climbed out of the helicopter onto the surface of the glacier. As he hurried away, he turned back and waved to Luke and Ezzy. They waved back.

Soon the helicopter was back in the air, headed north. Luke grabbed Ezzy's hand and applied his surprisingly strong small boy death grip. She tried to look more confident than her stomach felt. Luckily, it was a short flight to a landing area at the airport.

By the time Ezzy and Luke had climbed out of the helicopter, a mini-bus had screeched to a halt nearby. Anders, from the Arctic Palace, hopped out. As the helicopter rose and flew away, Ezzy and Luke waved to the pilots.

Ezzy approached Anders and whispered, "My brother's not feeling so good. You might want to take it easy on the ride back to the hotel."

Anders smiled. "Sure, no problem. Besides, I know a short cut."

Given their last experience with Anders driving, Ezzy had to wonder exactly what kind of short cut he had in mind. But she didn't want to embarrass Luke

by saying anything more or seem scared herself. "I've...
uh... got shotgun," she called out before climbing into
the front passenger seat.

Anders' short cut was on a dirt road that was
more potholes than actual road. To avoid potential tire-
swallowers, he swerved the mini-bus back and forth.
Ezzy hesitantly twisted around. Sitting behind her, Luke
had a tourniquet-tight grip on her seat's headrest, and
his expression suggested he'd rather be swimming in
the fjord's ice-cold water than riding in the mini-bus
with Anders driving. Luke's skin tone had also turned
another disturbing shade of green. Ezzy decided it was
something akin to guacamole gone bad.

If Luke barfs, Ezzy thought, *I'll be in the direct line
of fire.* Calling shotgun and sitting in front of him had
suddenly become a very, very bad move. "You doin'
okay back there, buddy?"

Luke closed his eyes and groaned.

"How much further is it?" Ezzy asked Anders.

"Not too far, I can go a little faster if you want."

"No!" Luke and Ezzy shouted simultaneously.

They weaved their way over a small hill. Anders
then steered the mini-bus onto a paved road running
around the perimeter of a large fenced-in property.

"What's in there?" Ezzy asked.

Anders slowed and pointed to several tall red and
white towers in the distance belching steam. A few in-
dustrial looking gray buildings sat nearby. "That's the
geothermal power plant."

"Geothermal? Like heat from underground?" Luke mumbled.

"Yup," Anders answered. "We're trying to go one hundred percent geothermal and wind, but we're not there yet."

"Hey," Ezzy said. "Is that why the glacier here is melting so fast? Because of geothermal heat?"

Anders shrugged. "Nah, the scientists don't think so. It's really far down, and under the glaciers it's not as hot as it is here."

Anders turned off the pavement and onto another dirt road full of holes. It took them over a low but steep hill and then onto the main thoroughfare. Minutes later, they arrived at the Arctic Palace hotel. "*Voilà*," Anders said with a flourish. "Here we are, safe and sound."

Ezzy jumped quickly out of the van in case Luke was about to let loose. "Safe yes, not so sure about sound."

Luke climbed out more slowly. "No more short cuts."

Hendrik strode out from the hotel. "We've been expecting you two." He led Ezzy and Luke inside to the restaurant. As they ate lunch, Hendrik asked about their hike and reported that their father would be going in the helicopter with the injured researcher to the hospital.

"Who got hurt?" Ezzy asked.

"I'm afraid it was Dr. Dixon. Her rope seems to have split and she fell into a large moulin. Luckily there was a ledge not too far down."

"Is she going to be okay?" Luke asked.

"We think so. But we're so glad your dad was there to help. I expect you'll hear from him soon. He should be able to call your room directly from the hospital or your phone if you have international service."

"How did her rope break?" Ezzy asked, thinking about how the researchers had talked about the importance of safety and checking their equipment.

Hendrik paused noticeably before answering. "Weird things happen on the ice and in the cold. And as I said before, it's dangerous working up on the glacier."

A man with a worn baseball cap pulled low over his face and head tilted down approached the table. He carried a toolbox and whispered something into Hendrik's ear.

"Thank you, I'll get right on it," said Hendrik in response. "Kids, this is Anguk. He's the one that really keeps this place going. Can fix just about anything. He'll show you to your room. I've got a phone call I need to take."

Anguk looked up at Ezzy and Luke. It was Katya's father. The steely expression on his face suggested he'd prefer to feed them to his dogs rather than take them to their room. He grudgingly waved them forward. At their room, the man watched silently as they unlocked the door with the card key their father had given them and went in.

Once inside, Ezzy turned to Luke. "Katya's dad is kinda creepy."

"Yah. Maybe he doesn't like kids or something."

"Maybe."

*   *   *

Puppy Trouble

Ezzy made sure her cell phone was fully charged, on, and had service. On the trip, it was only for emergencies or taking photos. Her dad said that international calls and even texting were expensive. Besides, as he mentioned on their hike, he wanted her to be present, living in the moment, and not spending all her time on the phone.

"How long do you think Dad will be?" Luke asked.

Ezzy shrugged. "I don't know."

Luke grabbed one of the books they'd brought along. It was an adventure story about a boy who could talk to sharks. He jumped onto his bed to read and Ezzy scooted in next to him. Ten pages into the story, they heard shouting from outside. Ezzy and Luke jumped up to look out the window. The young girl they'd met before, Katya, was standing next to an older boy. The two of them appeared to be arguing.

"C'mon," Luke said. "Let's go out."

Luke and Ezzy ran out of the room and through the back door of the hotel. They headed toward Katya. She saw them approaching and said, "Hey."

First thing Ezzy noticed about the boy was—the gun. He had a rifle held casually over his shoulder. He was lean and tall, with dark hair and a wide ruddy face with a small scar across his chin. He eyed them warily and said to Katya, "You mak'n friends with foreigners again."

"They're guests. Be nice, Malik."

"Why should I? Don't know them, don't care." He then looked directly at Ezzy. "What's that thing around your neck? Some kind of weird animal die or what?"

Ezzy fingered her purple scarf and glared at the boy.

"Don't pay any attention to my brother," Katya told her.

"Whatever," Malik said. "But you'd better get that pup back or Dad will have your hide. Can't even hold onto a little, itty bitty puppy."

"Aren't you supposed to be meeting Dad?" Katya responded.

"Yeah, yeah... we're going seal hunting. Aiming right for the eyes." Malik raised his eyebrows at Ezzy and

Luke, pretending like he was going to shoot in the direction the puppy had run. Katya's brother then strode off toward the coast.

"Jerk!" Katya yelled after him. She turned to Ezzy and Luke. "Dante got loose again chasing another bird. He went that way." She sprinted in the direction the puppy had gone. "Dante! Dante!"

Ezzy and Luke ran after her. "Here, Dante!"

Katya stopped and spun around, searching the area. "He couldn't have gone far." Then she stared at what was to her left—the road. "Oh no."

There wasn't much traffic but still the road posed a real danger to the puppy. Katya called out again, an expression of dread on her face. Ezzy and Luke followed as she walked to the edge of the pavement.

They stood silently, scanning the road and rocky area around the hotel. Ezzy heard a faint yip coming from across the road. Katya must have heard it too and after looking both ways, she ran across the pavement. Ezzy and Luke followed. Again, they heard the plaintive call. It was a little louder now. They climbed over the rocks adjacent to the road. Still no sign of Dante. The boardwalk to the Kangia Icefjord was nearby. Avoiding a large mud hole, Katya ran to it and clambered up. Ezzy and Luke were right behind her.

"Dante!" Katya called.

From almost directly in front of them came a tiny but distinct bark. On the other side of the boardwalk lay a steep-sided ditch at least three feet deep. Surrounded by grass, it was hard to make out. From atop the boardwalk, however, they could see the hole and what lay at the bottom—a dirty, shivering puppy.

"Dante," muttered Katya.

The puppy looked up and whimpered.

Katya jumped off the boardwalk and stepped to the edge of the ditch. The soft dirt began to give way. Before she fell in, Katya leapt back onto the boardwalk.

The puppy let out a strident yip and pawed at the wall of the ditch. Dirt fell away and onto the small dog.

"Stop, Dante!" Katya yelled. "Stop!"

Luke turned to Ezzy. "What should we do?"

"I'll try to reach him." Ezzy lay down on the boardwalk and reached over the edge into the ditch. But either the hole was too deep, or her arm was too short. She couldn't reach the trembling, mud-covered puppy.

"What now?" Luke asked.

Ezzy looked around. No one else was in sight. The shivering puppy let out another plaintive cry.

Luke inched closer to the edge of the boardwalk as if he was going to jump down. Ezzy pulled him back just as more dirt crumbled into the ditch. "Don't want you falling in too."

Then Ezzy remembered the other day and how Dante had tugged playfully on Luke's shoe. She had an idea. Ezzy unwrapped the purple scarf from around her neck. She tossed one end into the ditch and shook it gently. "Here Dante! Get the scarf!"

The puppy looked up at the girl and then tentatively mouthed the fuzzy purple scarf.

"Wiggle it some more," Luke urged.

Ezzy gently shook the scarf and pretended to pull it away. The puppy leapt onto the end and grabbed the scarf in its teeth.

"That's it," encouraged Ezzy.

"Pull, Dante!" Katya ordered.

The puppy shook his head and the scarf, growling playfully. Ezzy pulled on the scarf and the puppy pulled back. Then she slowly began to draw the scarf up along the side of the ditch.

"Don't let go," shouted Luke. "Hang on!"

About halfway up, the wall of the ditch began to give way again. The puppy let go of the scarf and fell, landing in the wet mud, coated with dirt.

"Dante!" Katya called out.

"Try again," Luke said as the furry little dog shook, and dirt and mud went flying.

Ezzy lowered the scarf again so that it was touching the puppy's nose. "Get the scarf!" Ezzy urged, wiggling it. "Get the scarf. Good dog."

The wet, mud-streaked, dirt-speckled puppy grabbed the purple scarf and tugged. Ezzy pulled back. The little dog held on. She began again to pull him up.

"Hang on, Dante," Katya called. "Don't let go!"

Ezzy drew the scarf in a little faster this time, praying the puppy would hang on. About halfway up, Dante began to whimper. Ezzy kept pulling. Dirt fell into the ditch. *Hang on,* Ezzy thought, *just a little further.* A tiny snout and mouth gripping the scarf appeared. Then Dante popped out of the ditch. As soon as he was clear, Katya reached down and grabbed him. She hugged the puppy tight. "Good dog! Good dog." She paused. "I mean bad dog, bad dog. No more chasing birds!"

Katya handed the puppy to Luke and hugged Ezzy. "Thank you so much. That dog is a little devil and always getting into trouble. You saved him."

Hugging the now mud-streaked girl, Ezzy silently thanked her mother for the scarf.

Just then a clump of grass that had been stuck to one side of the ditch broke off and fell in with a thump. More dirt collapsed into the hole.

As Luke handed the puppy back to Katya, he stared at the wall of the ditch. "Hey, what's that?" He bent down to look closer.

Katya and Ezzy leaned down to see as well. The collapse of more dirt had exposed something brown and shiny.

Ezzy leaned even closer. "It's a pipe."

Luke rolled his eyes. "I know *that.* But what's it for? Did it cause the hole?"

Katya stared at the pipe. "Nah, the hole is probably because of the thawing permafrost."

"What exactly is permafrost?" Ezzy asked.

"That's when the ground is frozen," Luke answered. "I read about it before we came. When it thaws, it gets all muddy and stuff."

"Yeah," said Katya. "And the roads get all bumpy and we get big holes and ditches in the ground."

"What's the pipe for, then?" Luke asked.

Katya stared at it. "I don't know. Probably something to do with the construction of the new spa or boardwalk."

"New spa?" Ezzy asked.

"Yeah," Katya answered, pointing to the building under construction a little to the north.

"We should take a photo of the ditch and tell someone," Luke suggested. "So like, no one falls in, or the walkway collapses or something."

From the inside pocket of her fleece vest, Ezzy pulled out her phone. She'd grabbed it as they ran out of their room in case their father called. Turning the phone sideways to get the best view of the ditch, she took a photo. Then she snapped another one that showed the exposed pipe. "Got it."

With Katya carrying the puppy, the three of them headed back toward the Arctic Palace.

"Is Malik, your brother, really going to shoot a seal?" asked Luke.

"I doubt it," Katya answered. "It's getting harder and harder to find them these days. Less ice and all."

"But wouldn't he feel bad about killing it?"

"My dad says it's an important part of our history and we honor the seal by using every part of it, meat for food, hide for clothing and things."

"I could never kill one," Luke told her.

Katya nodded and led them behind the hotel where a pen had been set up for the puppies. She put Dante inside with the others and made sure the gate was securely locked.

Just then, a burping noise came from inside Ezzy's vest. Katya turned to her in surprise. With a sheepish grin, Ezzy pulled out her cell phone. "Hi Dad, is everything okay?" She put it on speaker so Luke could hear too.

Ezzy's father quickly filled them in, explaining that the scientist Maggie had fallen into a deep hole in the ice. Her leg was fractured in several places and she had badly bruised ribs. Because of the quick response, she was expected to make a full recovery. The scientist had insisted her partner, Dr. Johnson, stay out and continue their research so Dr. Skylar wanted to stay overnight with her to keep her company and be sure no complications arose. "Is that okay with you guys?"

"Sure, Dad. No problem," said Ezzy. "I can take care of Luke."

"I know you can, but I've spoken with Hendrik and he's going to have someone regularly check in on you."

"I'm not a little kid, Dad," Ezzy said. "We don't need a babysitter."

"Yeah," Luke said into the phone.

"Humor me, guys," he replied. "You're in a foreign country. It would make me feel much better knowing you were both being looked in on."

Ezzy rolled her eyes and nodded. "Okay, I get it. When will you be back?"

"Sometime in the morning, I think. Take care of each other and stay out of trouble. And leave your phone on in case I call. And you can call me anytime if you need me."

"Thanks, Dad, we'll be fine," Ezzy said. "See you tomorrow."

"Bye, Dad," Luke added. "Don't worry."

Ezzy ended the call.

Katya turned to Ezzy. "I gotta run and get the food ready for the dogs."

"Do you need any help?" Luke asked.

"Nah, it's really stinky work, part of my chores. Besides, Dad wouldn't want you back there."

"We'll show Hendrik the ditch," Ezzy told her.

"Okay, cool. See ya later. And thanks again for saving Dante," Katya told them before leaving.

Ezzy and Luke watched her leave and then headed back to the hotel. They climbed the stairs to a deck behind the hotel. A few people were sitting around small tables sipping drinks. Turning back toward the coast, Luke pointed out another iceberg floating by. "Kinda looks like a big hat."

Ezzy turned to see the iceberg and discovered a part of the hotel she hadn't noticed before. It was roped off and also under construction.

A door nearby creaked open. "Ah ha. There you two are!"

Walking toward them were Hendrik and his wife SL. Ezzy inhaled deeply before stinky perfume contaminated the air. This time the woman had on high heels, tight leather leggings and a thigh-length white cowl-neck sweater. The large earrings she had on matched a bracelet of big pearls. Ezzy unconsciously smoothed her hair and fleece vest. Behind the couple skulked Anguk, Katya's father, eyeing them guardedly.

"I see you've found our expansion," Hendrik told them. "We're adding another fifty rooms."

"And the spa on the other side of the road," SL added. "We'll be the first five-star hotel in the area, maybe even the country."

Hendrik chuckled. "Well, we'll be the only one here with a spa at least."

Ezzy tried to stifle a sneeze, but it was no use. The woman's perfume was like sneeze-o-matic.

"Oh my, bless you," SL said. "Allergies?"

Ezzy blushed. "Something like that."

"Have you spoken with your father?" Hendrik asked.

"Yeah," Ezzy said. "He just called."

"Right, then you know he's staying at the hospital tonight."

Ezzy and Luke nodded.

"We've got an iceberg tour and whale watching boat going out first thing in the morning. Would you two like to go?"

"That would be awesome," Luke said.

"Uh, if it's okay with our dad?" Ezzy added.

"I already spoke to him about it. He said it would be fine. It's one of the excursions we regularly offer our guests." Hendrik continued, telling Ezzy and Luke what to wear and where to go after breakfast to meet the shuttle to the dock. "As for dinner tonight, you're welcome to join us and some guests or go on your own. It'll be on me for all that your father's doing. Have whatever you want."

"Thanks," replied Ezzy. "Maybe we'll just go on our own, if that's okay." She thought it would be kinda cool and very grown up for her and Luke to eat in the restaurant by themselves. And besides, if she sat with SL asphyxiation was a very real possibility.

"Sure thing," said Hendrik. "I'll let them know you'll be coming in. Enjoy."

Ezzy was about turn away and head back to their room when she remembered about the ditch. "Oh yeah," she said. "Almost forgot." She was about to say that one of Katya's puppies fell into the ditch, but then realized maybe the girl's father would be mad Dante had gotten loose. "We... uh... found a ditch across the road." She pulled out her phone.

Hendrik leaned in for a closer look. "Oh, and so close to our boardwalk. Thank you, we'd better get that fixed."

Luke pointed to a shiny glare in the image. "There was a pipe in it too. Maybe it was what caused the hole."

"More likely that darn thawing permafrost," said SL. "But thank you for telling us. Anguk can fix it. Here, let me show him." She took the phone from Ezzy's hand. As she turned to show Anguk, the phone slipped from the woman's grasp. SL twisted trying to catch it and stumbled. As the phone hit the floor one of her stiletto heels came down, stabbing the case like a stake to a vampire's chest. "Oh dear!" she cried out.

Hendrik steadied his wife as Ezzy grabbed the phone from the floor.

"I am *so* sorry," SL said, standing up and smoothing her clothes. "I hope it's not damaged."

Ezzy wiped off the face of the phone and checked to see if it was still working. "No worries. Dad made us buy these special extra tough cases so they wouldn't break even if we dropped them."

"Oh, thank goodness," SL said smiling. "That was very smart of him. Right, Anguk?"

"Yes, ma'am," he muttered.

Ezzy showed the handyman the photo but held onto the phone. "Here's the ditch."

Anguk nodded, turned, and began walking away.

"Don't you want to know where it is exactly?" Ezzy asked.

"I know the area," he grunted back at them.

Hendrik and SL said goodbye and that they hoped Ezzy and Luke would enjoy dinner and the boat ride. Hendrik also gave them a number on the hotel phone to call his direct line in case they needed anything.

A little while later, as Ezzy was unlocking the door to their room, she turned to Luke. "Yup, Katya's father definitely gives me the creeps."

"Maybe he doesn't like his job or something," Luke offered.

"Maybe."

Once inside the room, Ezzy thought of her dad and suggested they wash up before dinner. She was looking forward to going on their own. It felt very grown up. And the boat ride in the morning to see icebergs and whales sounded pretty good too. Though she was a little surprised her father was letting them go on their own. He'd been pretty protective ever since last summer's near-death adventure. From outside came a symphony of eerie howls. "Must be feeding time."

*   *   *

Icebergs and Whales, Oh My

For dinner, Ezzy and Luke sat at a small square table for two. The staff waited on them as if they were celebrities, giving them heaping plates of French fries and all the soda and lemonade they could drink. Hendrik and SL came by to say hello and introduced their dinner guests. It was their group of potential investors. Ezzy was glad they'd opted for dinner on their own instead of with a bunch of boring strangers. Besides, SL had on enough perfume to take down an elephant.

After dinner, Ezzy and Luke were provided a choice of movies to watch on the television in their room along with an unlimited supply of popcorn through room service. They decided on a double feature so they each could pick a film. Luke chose *Finding Nemo* and Ezzy went for *Captain Marvel*. Soon after the start of the second film both were sound asleep.

*   *   *

The next morning, after breakfast, Ezzy and Luke met Anders in the hotel parking lot. He drove them and a group of other guests to the nearby inlet. Ezzy expected Anders to say goodbye and return to the hotel. Instead, he grabbed a backpack and led the group to a forty-five-foot powerboat tied up alongside a nearby dock.

"You're coming with us?" Ezzy asked.

"I'd better be. I'm driving."

"You're... the captain?" Ezzy stammered. "Are you old enough?"

Anders laughed. "I'm older than I look. Besides, I grew up on boats back home in Denmark. And heck, these days, on autopilot, boats can just about steer themselves."

That didn't make Ezzy feel any more confident in Anders seafaring skills. The expressions on the faces of the other hotel guests, a family of four and an older couple, suggested they were dubious as well.

The orange-hulled boat had a V-shaped bottom and white superstructure. Waiting for them at the rail stood a young woman with an athletic build and glowing tan skin. Her long, wavy, brown hair was streaked with blonde and tied back in a messy ponytail. She wore a red fleece-lined windbreaker with matching pants. Ezzy thought she was exactly what an outdoor adventure guide should look like.

"Hey," the young woman said. "Welcome aboard. I'm Elise. Step right on up and make your way onto the boat. First thing up will be a safety briefing inside the cabin."

Anders hopped aboard. "Folks, follow Elise and I'll see you in a few minutes. A couple of those captainy things I need to do."

Ezzy and Luke followed the others. Left on their own to dress that morning, they'd worn comfortable sneakers, since they weren't going hiking, along with jeans, long-sleeved shirts, and their fleece vests. They'd also brought along their hats, gloves, and puffy coats. Ezzy's purple scarf was mud-covered from the ditch incident the day before, so she'd replaced it with one that was black and white striped with fringe.

Inside the covered cabin, the guests sat on gray metal benches alongside tables, both of which were bolted to the floor. Ezzy could think of only one reason why the tables and benches would be so firmly secured. Waves and rolling. Luke had been fine last summer on a ship, but with his recent tendency to get motion sick, she hoped seasickness wasn't next on his puke-inspiring activities list. Stretching her neck, Ezzy strained to see out the rectangular windows lining the cabin.

Elise soon swept in and stood in front of the group. She put on a slim headset and tapped the small lip microphone in front of her mouth. "Can you all hear me?"

"Yes!"

"Great. Well, hello again, and welcome aboard the M/V *Ice Maiden 2.*"

"Wonder what happened to the *Ice Maiden 1*?" Luke whispered to Ezzy.

She chuckled quietly and put a finger to her lips.

"Before we leave the dock, just a few safety items to go over. The lifejackets and survival suits are stored in the boxes on the stern or back deck. In an emergency, that's where we'll muster."

"Survival suits?" Luke whispered to Ezzy.

Elise must have heard as she winked at Luke and added, "Don't worry, we've never had to use them. This is a very safe boat and Anders is a fine captain. But in case of fire or if we need to abandon ship, again, muster on the stern deck. We are also equipped with two life-rafts big enough to hold everyone. Please be careful as you make your way around the boat. One hand for you and one hand for the boat. We have a head below for your use, that's the bathroom, but please do not flush anything other than #1, #2, or toilet paper. There's also water, juice and coffee available as well as some snacks for later. Any questions?"

One of the kids in the family, who looked about six to Ezzy, raised his hand.

Elise smiled. "Yes?"

"How close will we get to the icebergs? Can we go out on one?"

Elise chuckled. "We'll get pretty close. But no, we cannot go onto any of the icebergs or get too close. They can be unstable, and pieces often break off, which can be dangerous and create big waves."

Luke raised his hand. "Will we see whales?"

"I sure hope so," Elise answered.

"Okay, if you have any other questions, please do not hesitate to ask myself or Anders. And you're welcome to go up to the bridge once we are underway."

Anders came through a doorway at the head of the cabin. "Everyone all set? Any last requests... I mean questions?" He laughed.

There were a few nervous chuckles and no additional questions. Anders turned to Elise. "Okay then, get ready to cast off."

The young captain went forward and soon the engine rumbled to life. Elise cast off the dock lines and the boat cruised slowly out toward the open sea. It was partly cloudy with a breeze out of the east. Once outside the inlet, the temperature dropped due to the wind blowing over the cold Arctic ocean and nearby ice. The crisp air smelled like the sea with a mix of saltiness and seaweed.

It took about twenty minutes to reach the first iceberg. To get the best view, Ezzy and Luke, along with the other passengers, moved to the starboard rail on the stern deck. The iceberg floated about fifty feet away on a slightly choppy green-blue sea. With a V-shaped depression at its center, the iceberg resembled a giant thirty-foot-tall frozen bowtie.

"Awesome," exclaimed Luke. "Take a photo, sis."

Ezzy pulled out her phone and focused on the iceberg. She took a shot and then handed it to Luke. "Here, you take a few."

"Cool," Luke said, training the phone's camera on the big floating bowtie. "Check out the waterfall at the center."

At the iceberg's midpoint a narrow stream of meltwater cascaded into the sea.

Elise's voice rang out through speakers on the stern deck. "This time of year, especially during the daytime, the ice is melting. Unfortunately, it's not safe for us to get any closer due to the danger of ice falls. But we'll take a slow cruise around the berg for an ice-max 360 view... get it IMAX, icemax." They could hear her snickering over the intercom.

As the boat made its way around the iceberg, Ezzy noticed how the sun illuminated the surface causing it to gleam brightly, but also created grayish blue shadows under overhangs. At the iceberg's base, sunlight reflecting off the ocean made it glow green.

Luke abruptly twisted around and stared at the other side of the boat. "Did you hear that?"

"Hear what?" Ezzy asked.

Luke ran across the deck. Ezzy went after him, while everyone else remained where they were, viewing the iceberg. At the rail on the other side of the ship, Luke leaned over to look below. Ezzy joined him and leaned over too.

A spout of water erupted, dousing Ezzy and Luke. Ezzy froze, open-mouthed while Luke simply giggled and pointed down. "Whale!"

Ezzy wiped off her face and groaned, "And I thought iguana boogers in the Galápagos were bad. Whale snot, yuck!"

"C'mon Ez," Luke said. "That was so cool. It's just a little water. And look, there's the whale."

Ezzy peered more cautiously over the rail. The grayish-black bumpy surface of a whale was sliding by. As it dove, the whale's wide tail fluke slid silently underwater.

"Hey, folks!" announced Elise over the intercom. "We've got a humpback whale off the port side, that's the left."

The other passengers scrambled over and crowded in beside Ezzy and Luke. A few moments later, about fifteen feet away, a wide geyser-like spout shot skyward.

"There!" Luke shouted, pointing.

"Watch closely, folks," Elise added. "Humpbacks are baleen whales, meaning they sieve food out of the sea with big plates in their mouths. They feed on plankton, small fish, squid, and krill. They're also the acrobats of the whale world. Keep your eyes out and let's hope it'll give us a show."

Coming to the surface, the whale spouted again. And as it dove, the humpback flapped its tail fluke.

"Did you see the black and white color and pattern on the underside of the tail fluke?" Elise asked. "Each humpback has a different pattern, like a fingerprint, so we can tell them apart. That one was Dementor. One of our local researchers is a giant Harry Potter fan and thought the black markings on his tail fluke looked like the ghostly dementors from the stories." She laughed.

Then, a little further away, the whale leapt high out of the water. More than half its huge body went air-borne, including its long white flippers. Crashing down, the whale created a colossal splash. People on the deck jumped back to avoid getting drenched.

"Awesome!" exclaimed Luke.

"Wow! Dementor sure knows how to put on a show," Elise noted for the crowd. "We think breaching may be a way whales communicate, as sound travels a long way underwater. Then again, maybe they're just having fun."

"Do it again!" someone shouted.

The group watched in suspense, clearly hoping the whale would breach again.

"Also, keep your eyes out for bubbles. Humpbacks are also known for their bubble-net feeding. As a group, they use their blowholes to create a ring of bubbles that rise to the surface and herd fish like a net. Then the whales come up underneath the bubble-net and gulp up big mouthfuls."

Everyone watched and waited, hoping for a follow-up leap or some big time bubble action. Two spouts gushed skyward as a pair of whales came to the surface side-by-side.

"Looks like Dementor found a friend," Elise told them. "Watch for the tail fluke. Let's see who it is. I have a chart of whales and their fluke patterns put together by scientists here in Greenland if you're interested."

The two whales dove simultaneously. Dementor's tail fluke slid smoothly underwater, but just before submerging the other whale gave a little tail waggle. The underside of its tail fluke was mostly black with a thick white line across the middle.

Elise joined the group on the stern deck. "Anyone guess that whale's name?"

No one answered.

"It's Oreo," she told them. "Also known as Double-Stuff."

Luke and Ezzy laughed along with the rest of the guests.

"In addition to humpbacks," Elise announced. "We often see minke or fin whales this time of year."

To better observe the whales, Anders had stopped

the boat. Now he began slowly cruising again around the iceberg. Everyone continued to watch for the whales from the port side. When Dementor and Oreo failed to make another appearance, the group headed to the starboard rail for a better view of the iceberg.

With the breeze and some clouds, it was cold on the stern deck. Now bundled up in their coats, Ezzy and Luke huddled close for extra warmth.

As the boat came around the other side of the big bowtie iceberg, three smaller chunks of ice bobbing up and down came into view. One was the size of a car, while the other two were more on the scale of scooters. The boat slowed. Ezzy leaned over the railing to see better. There were fractures and crannies in the ice chunks as if carved out by a giant ice-cream scoop. Meltwater trickled over little ledges in the ice.

"Pardon me," Elise said stepping up to the rail beside Ezzy. She held a long pole with a net on the end.

"What's that for?" Luke asked.

"Watch and see."

The young woman leaned over, lowered the net, and smoothly scooped up a piece of ice about the size of a loaf of bread. It was perfectly transparent. Ezzy hadn't even noticed it. Elise lifted the ice into the boat and dumped it onto the deck. "Anyone for an iceberg slushie?"

She took a pocketknife from her jacket and began hacking off small shards of ice. Anders appeared with a stack of paper cups. Elise put several shards of ice in each cup and began passing them around. "This ice melted and then refroze. That's why it's so clear. Best tasting water you'll ever drink."

Ezzy and Luke each received a cup. Most of the ice had already melted. Ezzy took a sip. Even though she had never really thought about how water tasted, she decided it was coldest, freshest, and best tasting H_2O she'd ever had.

"How come it's not salty?" someone asked.

"When seawater first freezes much of the salt remains in the sea. When it melts and refreezes it's pure freshwater."

"You should bottle it!" another person suggested.

"In some places they actually do that," Anders responded. "There are also some people who want to sell our icebergs for freshwater, especially with the glacier and ice shelf breaking up faster than ever."

"Because of climate change," Luke added.

"That's right," Anders continued. "Some people even want to tow the icebergs away."

Ezzy suddenly realized their captain was on the stern deck. "Hey, who's driving the boat?"

"What?" Anders asked with concern. "Ha... just kidding. It's on autopilot, and I've got a dynamic positioning system that keeps us in place automatically."

From off in the distance came the sound of a puttering engine. Anders went to the rail and looked forward toward the bow. "Looks like we've got company.

Better put my captain hat back on and head to the bridge."

Ezzy, Luke, and the other passengers went to the rail to look for themselves. A small boat or dinghy with an outboard engine and one man driving at the stern was approaching the *Ice Maiden 2*.

When the dinghy neared, Ezzy turned to Luke. "Hey, I think it's Katya's dad."

"Yeah," Luke said. "And as usual he doesn't look very happy."

The small boat pulled alongside the *Ice Maiden 2*. Luke was right, Ezzy thought. Speaking into a small handheld radio, Anguk's expression suggested he was either miserable or mad, or maybe both.

Minutes later, Elise approached the two Skylars. "Ezzy and Luke? Right?"

"Yes," Ezzy answered.

"Anguk from the hotel is here to pick you up," Elise told them. "Your dad is back at the hotel and wants you to join him."

"Really?" Ezzy said, wondering why he hadn't called her phone, which she removed from an inside pocket of her jacket.

Elise glanced at the phone. "Won't get any signal out here."

"Oh, okay. Ah... how do we get in the small boat?"

"Follow me. It's easy."

Ezzy and Luke followed Elise to the opposite side of the boat. She unlatched a small door in the railing and swung it open. It was where they had boarded from the dock. From a nearby box, the young woman removed a rope ladder and attached it to the deck so that it hung down alongside the boat's hull. Anguk then steered the dinghy so that it sat directly beneath the ladder.

"You want us to climb down?" Ezzy asked hesitantly.

"It's simple," Elise responded. "We do it all the time. Just hold onto the sides of the ladder and go backward slowly down. Anguk will keep the boat steady and help you in."

Ezzy looked at Luke. "You okay with this?"

Luke smiled. "This I can do. It's cars and helicopters that I have a problem with."

Ezzy thought about falling into the ocean and wondered if maybe they should put on lifejackets. But she didn't want to suggest it and sound like a scared little kid. Besides, this was the braver Ezzy, at least kind of.

"C'mon sis," Luke encouraged. "I'll go first."

The other passengers watched with interest as Luke grabbed hold of the ladder, turned around, and began slowly climbing down.

"Take your time," Elise told him. "No rush."

Luke easily scrambled down and was soon just above the small boat. There it got a little trickier. But Anguk had made his way forward and now stood next to the ladder, holding it with one hand to keep the dinghy steady. With the other hand, he grabbed Luke's jacket, plucked him off the ladder, and swung the boy onto a bench seat in the boat.

Luke grinned and looked up at his sister. "See, no problem, sis. You can do it."

Ezzy stared at the frigid water, the small dinghy rocking gently, and the scowling man below. She willed herself to be brave, whispering, "I can do this."

Ezzy tried to emulate what Luke had done, but as she grabbed the ladder and turned backward to go down, her legs felt wobbly and her arms shook so much the ladder slapped loudly against the hull of the boat. She froze and could feel her face turning red.

"Ah... maybe we should get you a lifejacket just in case," Elise whispered.

Ezzy's face grew even hotter. She buried her nose in the scarf around her neck. From it came the faintest whiff of her mother. "No, I got this."

Ezzy took a deep breath and willed her legs to move. Still trembling, she headed down the ladder, silently repeating to herself that she could do it. When she was in reach, Anguk grabbed her coat. "I got you," he said gruffly.

In an instant, Ezzy was lifted off the ladder and placed next to Luke who said, "See, nothing to it."

"Yeah, nothing to it," she mumbled.

Elise pulled up the ladder. "Thanks for coming. Hope you enjoyed the trip. See you later." She and the rest of the guests waved as Anguk started the outboard engine and steered the dinghy away from the *Ice Maiden 2.*

Ezzy and Luke waved back. As they pulled away, Ezzy looked up and saw Anders staring at them from the bridge. He waved half-heartedly with an odd look, which she thought suggested either serious concern for their welfare or a bad case of constipation.

*   *   *

The Ocean Erupts

The first thing Ezzy took note of was the fact that they were now in a really small boat. The next thing she noticed was the gun. A rifle lay on the deck at the stern next to Anguk. She looked closer at Katya's father. He had a dark blue knit cap pulled down to his bushy eyebrows and again, the expression on his face suggested misery, anger or some mix of the two. Ezzy wondered if he was mad because he'd been sent to retrieve her and Luke. She guessed her father had changed his mind about them going on their own.

Ezzy continued to watch Anguk. Like changing gears on a mountain bike, he controlled their speed by turning a swivel on the handle to the outboard engine. To change direction, he pushed it away or pulled it toward him. As he drove, the man stared straight ahead as if she and Luke weren't even there.

With the big bowtie iceberg blocking the wind and waves, their dinghy cruised smoothly through the water. Ezzy stared up at the iceberg and realized how truly enormous it was. A small chunk breaking off would squash them like a bug or at least capsize their little boat. Ezzy searched the vessel for a survival suit or lifejacket. The only things in the boat, other than them and the gun, were a set of oars and a gas can. Safety first was clearly not number one on Anguk's rules to live by.

As they came out from behind the iceberg, small choppy waves and wind struck the dinghy, causing it to rock. Ezzy grabbed Luke with one hand and the gunwale or side with the other. She turned to get a look at the *Ice Maiden 2*, but it was now hidden behind the bowtie iceberg. She faced front again. The coast and village of Ilulissat were still far away. She couldn't wait to get there. Ezzy was ready to be back on land and out of the small boat driven by Katya's creepy father. But then the dinghy began to veer sharply to the right and away from the coast and the village.

"Hey," Luke said, pointing back toward Ilulissat. "The hotel's over there."

Anguk stayed silent and stared ahead as he steered them around the other side of the iceberg. His facial expression remained as frozen as the ice around them. They passed the iceberg and cruised southeast toward the mass of icebergs stranded at the mouth of the Kangia Icefjord.

"Hey," Ezzy said louder and looking directly at Anguk. "Why are we going this way?"

The man remained still and quiet, staring ahead.

"What's going on?" Luke whispered to Ezzy. "Where's he taking us?"

"I'm going to start yelling really *really* loudly if you don't answer me," Ezzy warned.

Anguk rolled his eyes and huffed loudly. "We're taking the scenic route. You wanted to see icebergs, so I'm showing you some more on the way in."

"Uh, that's okay," Ezzy stuttered. "We're supposed to meet our dad at the hotel. Let's just go there."

Anguk cranked on the handle of the outboard engine. The roar of the motor was deafening as the boat picked up speed. Luke stared questioningly at Ezzy. She felt helpless. What could she do? Was he kidnapping them? She looked around for someone to wave to for help, but the tour boat was completely out of sight and there weren't any other boats around.

Ezzy held Luke's hand as the dinghy continued toward the mouth of the icefjord. Soon a flotilla of ice chunks floated by, swept downstream by the outflowing tide. Ahead lay a mountainous jumble of giant icebergs. It was the strangle point for icebergs drifting out of the fjord. Anguk steered around the massive iceberg jam into a narrow area of open water between the ice and other side of the fjord.

Ezzy scanned the coast, hoping there might be people on the shore. But here the coast was even more remote, lined only by dark and desolate rocky cliffs. Now well protected from the wind, the ocean was calm, and they cruised steadily upstream.

After a while, the boat began to slow. Anguk put the engine into neutral and they glided to a stop. Ezzy looked up. The bow was frighteningly close to the jumble of enormous icebergs.

"Now kids, *those* are some icebergs? How about a selfie with the icebergs for your papa? That's what they call them photos, *right?*"

Ezzy's eyes were wide as she glanced at Luke.

"Uh, it's only a selfie if we take it," Luke corrected. "And I thought we weren't supposed to get too close to the icebergs. It's dangerous."

The man grimaced. "Stop your whining. Give me your phone and I'll take a photo of you with the icebergs in the back."

"No, that's okay," Ezzy replied. "Let's just head back."

Anguk drew in an exasperated breath and seemed to glance toward the rifle at his feet. "Just give me the phone!"

Ezzy hesitated. "How about if I take a photo of all three of us?" From her pocket she pulled out her phone.

"No," snarled Anguk. "Give me the phone."

"Geez, no need to go postal on us," Ezzy returned. "Do you even know how to take a photo with a cell phone?"

In lieu of an answer, the man literally growled at them.

Luke nudged Ezzy with his elbow and nodded toward Anguk, encouraging her to give the man her phone.

"Okay, okay, if you want to do it that bad," Ezzy declared as she leaned toward Anguk with the phone in her outstretched hand.

Suddenly, the boat began to pitch. Giant bubbles erupted all around them as if the ocean had begun to boil.

Ezzy gasped. Was a volcano erupting underneath them? She had some experience with erupting volcanoes. She stared at the surrounding water. More bubbles rose to the surface. Soon they were in the middle of a ring of erupting bubbles. Hanging on to Luke, Ezzy leaned over and dared a look over the side. Something dark and massive was rising toward the surface. Before she could move back or even scream, a giant wide-open mouth came up right beside the boat. With a loud swoosh, the whale closed its mouth, gulping up a ton of water filled with squiggling little fish.

Nearby, another whale rose open-mouthed to the surface. Ezzy then felt a bump and their boat began to rise. A whale was coming up directly underneath them. Luke and Ezzy screamed as the little boat was launched upward. With the hand still holding her phone, Ezzy grabbed for the side of the boat. Simultaneously, Anguk lunged toward her. The boat tipped sideways. Anguk's outstretched hand knocked Ezzy's phone from her grip.

It flew out of the boat and right into the whale's mouth. In the moment all Ezzy's terrified brain could strangely think was that the whale was going to need smartphone dental floss or get terrible indigestion. Then she hoped it would spit out the phone. She watched for it, but the great behemoth submerged, presumably with her phone still in its mouth.

Their dinghy came down hard, tilted sharply to one side and nearly capsized. Ezzy fell into Anguk, knocking him backward. The man stumbled and she heard a scarily loud crack as Anguk's head struck the outboard engine. He slid down into the boat. As more bubbles erupted around them, Ezzy and Luke held on to one another and the boat, while Anguk lay unmoving in the stern.

The whales continued to surface to feed, and their little boat was shoved this way and that. Soon they were headed for the ice jam. Their boat was on a collision course with a massive iceberg.

Ezzy clinched her teeth, shut her eyes, and hugged Luke tight. She bent over him protectively, waiting for the impact. Seconds felt like hours until, with a sharp jolt, their small boat came to an abrupt halt. Ezzy opened her eyes and glanced nervously up at the ice. They hadn't crashed into the towering iceberg. Instead, they'd gotten stuck in a fracture in one that had been hard to see, floating only a foot or so above the sea surface.

Ezzy sighed with relief and released her brother. "You okay?"

He nodded. The two of them then turned to the man lying motionless in the stern.

"Is he dead?" Luke asked.

Ezzy looked closer. "No, I think he's just knocked out."

"What should we do?"

Ezzy glanced around and her eyes quickly landed on the man's rifle. She thought about how strangely he'd been acting.

"Why'd he want to take our picture so bad anyway?" Luke asked.

Ezzy had a sudden and disturbing thought. "Maybe he was trying to steal my phone."

"Really?"

She shrugged. "Yeah, remember what Dad said. It's hard to get things here and they're really expensive."

"But we'd tell everyone," Luke said.

"Maybe he thinks no one will believe us or he's going to make up some story about how I dropped it. Or maybe, he's planning on leaving us out here and make it look like an accident or something. Remember Hendrik said it's dangerous around here."

"For a phone?" Luke asked. "But he's Katya's father."

"Yeah, well I thought that guy John was nice in the Galápagos too. I'm not going to make that mistake again. People do bad things for money."

"What should we do?" Luke asked, staring at the man.

"I'm not sure," Ezzy replied. "But when he comes to, he might think I pushed him or something."

"It was an accident."

Ezzy nodded nervously, staring at the unconscious man and his rifle. "I know, but he might not think so. I'm gonna throw his gun overboard just in case."

The rifle lay only inches from Anguk's hand. Ezzy crept forward and reached for it. Just then, Anguk moaned and his eyes fluttered. Ezzy jumped back. The man lay still, but now his eyes were open and he was staring at her. If he'd seemed angry before, now he looked murderous.

Ezzy glanced around in panic. What should she do? If the man was up to no good, she had to protect Luke. She could try to hit the guy with one of the oars, but Ezzy didn't think she was strong enough to do any real damage. Besides, he had the gun. Groaning, Anguk started to sit up. The way Ezzy saw it, they had only one option.

Before she could think twice or change her mind, Ezzy climbed out of the boat onto the large, flat, low-lying iceberg they were stuck in. She turned to Luke. "C'mon!"

Luke hesitated until Anguk seemed to reach for the rifle. He then scrambled out of the boat and onto the iceberg beside Ezzy. She grabbed his hand. Together they ran across the ice, slipping and sliding along the way. All Ezzy could think about was getting away from Anguk and the gun.

Anguk woozily stood up in the dinghy. "Hey!" he shouted. "You kids get back here!"

Ezzy pulled on Luke and they leapt over a narrow gap onto an adjacent iceberg. She stopped and dared a look back. Anguk was yelling at them furiously. He then stepped out of the boat onto the ice. Under his weight, the iceberg tilted down. Anguk teetered before jumping back into the boat. He grabbed an oar and pushed on the ice, trying to release the dinghy from its grasp.

Ezzy had seen enough. She and Luke took off again, running across the fjord's frozen and floating surface. They came to a spot where a chunk of ice had fallen and created a narrow bridge. It led onto a nearby and much larger iceberg. Ezzy scrambled up onto the ice bridge. She began to crawl across. But then she stopped, thinking maybe she'd felt the ice beneath her move. Small shards of ice began falling from the underside of the bridge. Ezzy trembled and crawled faster than before. She reached the far side of the ice bridge and slid down on her butt. Standing, she turned to Luke. "C'mon, nothing to it. Like you always tell me."

Luke nodded and climbed up onto the frozen span of ice. He began to crawl across. Behind him, a crack appeared, and a larger chunk of ice fell from the underside of the bridge into the frigid water below.

"Hurry, Luke," Ezzy urged.

The ice creaked and moaned. A spiderweb of cracks appeared.

"Faster, Luke!"

The cracks widened and the whole ice bridge shook.

"Jump!" Ezzy shouted.

Luke pushed off and Ezzy reached out. Together they fell backward just as the bridge collapsed into the sea.

Getting to their feet, Ezzy and Luke jointly breathed a giant sigh of relief. In the distance, Anguk was still trying to shove the boat out from the ice.

"C'mon," Ezzy said. "Let's see if we can get across the ice to the other side of the fjord."

"But everyone said it's not safe on the icebergs," Luke told her.

"It's not safe with a creepy, angry guy in a small boat with a gun either."

Luke nodded.

The iceberg they were on sloped upward to a flat section topped by an enormous archway. Diffuse blue light shone down from under the arch. They scrambled up the slope. Ezzy was glad they had on gloves but wished they had worn their hiking shoes instead of sneakers. She and Luke made it to the top of the slope and paused in front of the archway. Cautiously, they crept forward. The archway led to as shadowy cave.

"Cool," said Luke, staring at the blue-striped walls of the cave.

A loud crack drew their attention back to the entryway as a refrigerator-sized chunk of ice broke off the arch and fell, blocking their path back.

"Guess we're going that way," Luke said, pointing toward a narrow vertical crack in the back wall of the cave.

Ezzy led the way, turning sideways to squeeze through. "Glad I'm not claustrophobic."

Luke followed, sucking in his stomach. "Yeah, but I wish I hadn't eaten so many French fries last night."

The two inched their way through the fracture. With the ice blocking the wind, it was warmer inside and a dim blue light lit the way. They used their gloves against the ice walls to brace themselves and balance on the slippery floor.

Up ahead, sunlight glinted off a stream of water trickling off the top of the iceberg. To exit the fracture, they'd have to pass through it. Ezzy braced herself and ducked under. Luke jumped through covering his head with his gloves.

They shook off the frigid water and looked around. Ezzy was relieved to see the other side of the fjord. But to get there, they were going to have to go across more ice. It was like a giant obstacle course made of floating, bobbing icebergs. Luckily, the icebergs were jammed in and mashed together, but still they'd need to find a safe route across. Luke pointed to their left. The iceberg there was higher than the one they were on but had a flat top like a giant table. Ezzy noticed what looked like notches or steps going up the iceberg. She nodded and they headed toward the big berg.

Ezzy boosted Luke up the first step-like notch in the ice. Then together, they began to climb. It was a pretty long way up to the surface, and they had to stop several times to rest. At the top, they caught their breath and looked for fractures or holes to avoid. Not seeing any, they headed across the surface of the iceberg. At the other edge, they found a smaller castle-like iceberg sitting only a few inches away. Ezzy readied to jump across. Then she felt something. A slight movement or shift in the icebergs. She stopped and listened, grabbing hold of Luke. Soon a thunderous whumpf rang out.

*   *   *

Back at the Ice Maze

Minutes later, Ezzy thanked whoever must be watching over them. After all, she and Luke had just narrowly escaped death by a high dive insta-freeze swim while experiencing an iceberg turned frozen bumper car tilt-o-wheel. She was also grateful she hadn't leapt onto the adjacent iceberg before all the action had started. Ezzy figured there must have been another big collapse at the glacier or ice shelf, and it had caused the waves that had moved through the fjord. Now that the icebergs had quieted, she and Luke once again searched for a safe route to the other side.

"C'mon, Luke," Ezzy urged. "This way." She took his hand to lead him onto another iceberg.

Luke pointed to her sneaker. "Your shoelace saved me back there."

Ezzy nodded as she bent down to retie her sneaker. They then crisscrossed the ice, going from one iceberg to another. In some places they had to crawl, in others they had to carefully climb down or navigate around fractures. In a few spots they slid down icy ramps on their bottoms. Some icebergs were too small or too unstable to walk across.

Luke shivered. "My feet are freezing."

"Mine too. But look, the other side isn't too much farther." Ezzy purposely didn't mention the area of open water between the jammed-in icebergs and shore.

They eventually reached the surface of a large iceberg that was barely above the water and as near to shore as they could get without swimming.

"Now what?" Luke asked.

"Good question," Ezzy replied, trying to figure how they were going to cross the frigid water without jumping in and going into hypothermic shock.

"Hmmm," muttered Luke, looking to their right with a scrunched up look on his face. He raised an eyebrow and almost smiled.

"What? What are you thinking?" Ezzy asked.

"See that iceberg. The one over there," he said, pointing back the way they'd come to an iceberg the shape of their dining room table at home, but a bit larger. "What if we get on it and paddle to shore."

"I don't know, it looks kinda tippy."

"Do you have a better idea?"

Ezzy shook her head. "Okay, let's check it out."

They worked their way back to the table/paddle boat-sized berg. Ezzy glanced about again, hoping to find another way to shore. Then she took a deep breath. "Guess it's our best option. I'll go first and see what happens."

"Maybe I should go," Luke countered. "I'm smaller."

"Yeah, but I'm older. I'll do it." Ezzy was determined to protect Luke even if she had to risk tipping over or falling in. She cautiously put a foot on the iceberg and pushed down lightly. It remained still. She put a little more weight on her foot and still the iceberg didn't move.

Ezzy then stepped cautiously onto the iceberg. She stood absolutely still as the iceberg sank a little and rocked gently. She inched further across. It seemed stable enough, but Ezzy's movement had caused the iceberg to start drifting away from the one Luke was on.

"Get on," Ezzy urged.

Luke jumped onto the iceberg, which caused it to bob up and down and rock from side to side. Ezzy dropped to her hands and knees to prevent sliding off. "I didn't say *jump* onto it."

Luke swayed and slid around on the ice. "Whoa. Whoa."

"Get down," Ezzy told him.

Luke fell to his hands and knees. "You didn't say *not* to jump. It was floating away!"

The two of them stayed still and waited for the iceberg to stop moving. It had floated into an adjacent iceberg, which helped.

"Okay, let's try to paddle to shore," Ezzy suggested.

Luke nodded and the two of them slid on their stomachs to the opposite sides of the iceberg. Once at their respective edges, each dipped a gloved hand into the water, and began to paddle. The iceberg rotated slightly and began to move.

"It's working," proclaimed Luke.

"Head for shore," Ezzy told him.

Luke paddled a little more before pulling his hand out and shaking it. "My fingers are numb."

"Hey, then at least you won't feel how cold it is."

"Ha... Ha."

"Just keep paddling," Ezzy urged. "It's not too far."

Slowly they made their way toward shore. Ezzy's hand was completely numb and her arm and shoulder ached, but she kept paddling. She turned to Luke. The determined look on his face and the fact that he continued to paddle even though he was freezing and must have been exhausted spurred Ezzy on. She paddled harder and looked for a landing area. "Aim for the mud."

Minutes later they felt a bump, and the iceberg was still. Ezzy rolled on her back and in one big exhalation, let out all the tension and fear she'd kept bottled up during their trek across the ice. Luke got onto his hands and knees, crawled over to Ezzy, and jumped on her. "We did it!"

The iceberg shuddered, and for a second Ezzy thought it would tilt over and dump them into the muck. But it remained firmly stuck in the mud. They hugged in joy and to warm up. Although Luke could totally annoy her at times and was often too smart for his own good, Ezzy really loved the kid. Shaking and rubbing her hands to get the feeling back, she said, "I'll go first."

Ezzy scooted on her butt to the edge of the iceberg and swung her legs off. She hopped off into the mud, sinking a few inches. Luke followed her. The two of them then slogged their way toward solid ground. Each time they lifted a foot out of the mud, it made a loud, wet, sucking noise.

Luke giggled. "You know what it sounds like?"

Ezzy rolled her eyes. "Don't even say it."

"Farts!" Luke laughed.

Ezzy laughed too and it felt good, even if they were exhausted, freezing, and still stuck out in the middle of nowhere.

The mud led to a beach blanketed by loose rocks. Ezzy scanned the area. They were in a small cove, surrounded by rocky cliffs.

Luke pointed up to their right. "There's some kind of shack up there. Maybe someone's there."

"Hello!" Ezzy called out.

"We're down here!" Luke added.

After a few more shouts and no response, they began searching the base of the cliff for a trail or some way to climb up. Ezzy noticed what appeared to be steam rising from the ground. It was at the base of the cliff beneath the shack. *That's weird,* she thought. She moved closer for a better look. It appeared as if there'd been a small landslide. Mist or steam seemed to be rising from a pile of dirt resulting from the collapse. Then Ezzy noticed something else. "Hey, come look at this," she said to Luke.

He joined her. "It's another pipe, like the one we saw in the ditch."

"It must come from the shack. Looks like it goes out under the mud to the water."

Luke backed away, puckering up his face. "Do you think they have a toilet up there? And that's well... a...a... poop chute?"

Ezzy couldn't help but chuckle. "That's totally gross, but I guess it could be." Then, given how freezing her hands were, she held them closer to the pipe. "It's warm, though."

Luke squeezed in next to her and put his hands near the exposed pipe as well. "Even if it is a poop chute," he said. "It feels *gooood.*"

Ezzy nodded. Once her hands had warmed up, she looked up at the shack. "C'mon, let's find a way up there."

They discovered a wide crack between the rocks that zigzagged up the cliff. It was a path, or close enough to one. Ezzy and Luke started up. It was a short but steep climb. In their exhausted state, it felt like an expedition up Mount Everest.

Reaching the top, Ezzy got a second wind, make that a third or fourth wind, and helped Luke up. They headed for the shack. It was a small green wooden hut with a sign out front, which Luke read, "Science Station Echo. Staff Only."

"I think we qualify for a pass right now," Ezzy told him, walking tiredly up several steps to the door. Shivering now, she knocked. No answer. She tried the doorknob. It was locked. "Maybe there's a back door."

Navigating around the rocks and a few muddy spots, they made their way to the back of the shack. Instead of a door, they found a large wooden box. The top was secured with a padlock.

"Hey," Luke said. "Maybe there's an extra key around like the one Dad leaves for us under the fake rock at home."

Ezzy shrugged, somewhat skeptical, and they began searching. She felt above the rim of the door at the front. No key there. Then she and Luke began checking rocks about the same size as their fake one at home. None were of the hollowed-out plastic variety.

Off to the side of the cabin was a small weather station. It had a tripod base with a tall pole outfitted with a solar panel, digital thermometer, and an anemometer to measure wind speed and direction. Luke went to take a closer look. "Ah ha!" He pulled a small magnetic box off from beneath the thermometer and slid the top back. Inside was a key.

"Brilliant," said Ezzy, who had been keeping an eye on her brother.

Luke unlocked the door and they went inside. First thing Ezzy did was look for a way to contact her father or anyone for help. Meanwhile, Luke found a couple of blankets. He gave Ezzy one and wrapped one around himself. There was no phone or radio, but Ezzy did discover a small stove. She turned a knob and a flame blossomed, bringing a surge of welcome warmth into the hut. They huddled close to the heat.

"Do you think there's anything to eat?" Luke asked. "I'm starved."

Above a small sink were a few cabinets. Ezzy searched the cabinets and found a half-filled jar of peanut-butter and some packets of quick-mix soup, oatmeal, and hot chocolate. She nearly drooled thinking of a cup of steaming hot cocoa. She turned the knobs next to the faucet, but nothing came out.

"Maybe you have to turn it on underneath," Luke suggested.

Ezzy nodded, bent down, and opened the cabinet below the sink. Inside were several pipes. A lever lay perpendicular to the pipe leading up to the sink. She tried to push it, but it didn't move. Then she tried pulling the lever and slowly it turned until it was parallel to the pipe. Ezzy stood up and turned the knob to the right of the spigot. Cold water began to trickle out. Soon a thin stream of water ran into the sink. Not wanting to put her hands in anymore cold water, Ezzy bent down and slurped directly from under the faucet. Luke came over and did the same.

"Cross your fingers," Ezzy said turning the other knob. The one she assumed was the hot water. Nothing came out. Then she noticed another spigot to the side of the faucet, wider with a pump action top. Ezzy crossed her fingers and pumped the top. At first nothing happened, but as more resistance built a trickle of steaming water appeared. Soon hot water flowed into the sink.

"Awesome!" Luke said. He found a cup in the cabinet above and grabbed a packet of hot chocolate. After mixing it with a spoon he'd found, Luke took a sip. His face lit up. "Mmmm, maybe the best hot cocoa ever."

"Or just the most needed," Ezzy chuckled. She made herself a cup and went to explore the cabin further. Luke seemed curious about the instant hot water maker and peered under the sink.

"Look at this," they said simultaneously.

Ezzy was at a desk that sat at the back wall below a window looking out over the icefjord. Mounted at the base of the window was a plaque, which Ezzy read, "Dedicated to the early explorers who risked life and limb to unveil the mysteries of Greenland's glaciers." A leather logbook lay on top of the desk. Ezzy scanned a few pages. "Looks like scientists come here on their way up to the glacier and record weather measurements."

"Cool," Luke replied. "There's a pipe under here that goes outside. Maybe the pipe we saw brings water up and it's heated by whatever's in that big box out back."

"Yeah, like the propane tank that Dad uses for our grill at home or something."

Luke glanced around and then paused with his scrunched-up-thinking-face. "But if the cold water is coming up, why was the pipe down there so hot?"

Ezzy shrugged. "I don't know. Let's have some soup."

They sat by the stove, wrapped in blankets drinking hot soup. Luke turned to Ezzy. "By the way, remind me never to do that again. No more iceberg hiking for me."

"Me either," Ezzy said. "I'll stick to look, but don't touch, walk, crawl or paddle from now on."

"What should we do now?" Luke asked.

"We need to find Dad and tell him what happened. Like about Anguk trying to steal my phone and threatening us."

A loud knocking on the door nearly shook the whole hut. Startled, Ezzy and Luke just about fell over.

The door swung open. Stepping into the hut with a smirk on his face and a rifle over his shoulder was Katya's brother, Malik. "Saw the door was open and wondered who was up here. You two lost or what?"

Ezzy was too surprised to answer. "Ah..."

"Actually, my father radioed saying you guys had jumped ship and there's a whole bunch of people out searching for you."

"Really?" Luke questioned.

"We didn't just jump ship," Ezzy responded. "Your dad threatened us with his gun and tried to steal my phone."

Malik stared at Ezzy like she had two heads. "What? Is that scarf around your neck too tight?"

"No really," Luke added. "He was mean, had a gun, and tried to take Ezzy's phone."

Malik shook his head. "You guys are bonkers. My dad is harmless. Besides, he would never hurt any of our precious tourists."

"I'm telling you he wanted my phone," Ezzy snapped.

"Yeah, well why would he get everyone out looking for you if that was true?"

Ezzy shrugged and muttered, "I don't know."

"By the way, you know you're not supposed to be in here," Malik told them. "How did you get in, anyway? You didn't break anything, did you?"

"Geez," Ezzy replied. "We could've died of hypothermia out there. I don't think anyone is going to care that we got in."

"Yeah," Luke added. "I found a key and we just made some hot chocolate and soup to get warm."

Malik looked at them suspiciously. "You didn't touch anything *else*, did you?"

"No," Luke responded.

"Well, I did turn on the stove," Ezzy added.

"Anything else?"

"We just looked around to get in and then got warm," Ezzy groaned. "What's your problem?"

"This place is off limits. Science stuff."

"Oh, for Pete's sake," Ezzy said. "Can you just help us get back to the hotel? My dad must be worried sick."

Malik removed a phone from the inside of his jacket. "I'll call back to the hotel to let them know I found you so they can call off the search. They can tell your dad. But gotta go outside for a signal." Malik walked out the door, turned his back to Ezzy and Luke and began speaking quietly into the phone.

"Lucky he came when he did," Luke told Ezzy. "And has a phone that works out here."

"Yeah, lucky," Ezzy said warily.

Malik returned. "I told them not to worry and that I'd bring you back to the hotel. No need for a big rescue helicopter or anything. It's not that far."

Luke frowned. "I could kinda go for a ride back."

"Oh, buck up, kid. A little hike won't hurt you."

"You have no idea what we've been through already," Ezzy responded sharply.

"Boo hoo," whined Malik. "I've got us a ride anyway. C'mon, help me put this place back in order and then I can get you two kiddies back to your daddy."

Ezzy wanted to strangle the guy, but then again, he knew the way back to the hotel. The three of them straightened up the inside of the shack. Luke rinsed out the cups they'd used, while Ezzy folded the blankets. Malik turned off the stove and the water under the sink. Closing the door, he took the key from Luke and locked it. He then put the magnetic key box back on the weather station.

"Do you come out here a lot?" Ezzy asked.

"Sometimes," Malik grunted.

Luke looked out over the cliff toward the icefjord. "We found a pipe down by the water."

"Yeah?" said Malik.

"We figured it brings water up to the shack," he added.

"And so?"

"It was hot and there was steam coming off it."

"Naah," Malik replied quickly. "It probably just felt warm. People always get weird when they've been out in the cold too long."

Ezzy shook her head. "No. It *was* hot and there *was* steam."

"I'm telling you, it's the ice. You were out there too long," Malik repeated. "The cold has seeped into your brains. C'mon."

Malik strode away, clearly expecting them to follow. But as he did, Ezzy noticed him glance back as if trying to look around the shack to the cliff below.

*   *   *

An All-Terrain Sled

E zzy and Luke struggled to keep up with Malik. Having spent his entire life hiking about the fjord, the older boy moved easily and swiftly across the rocks. Barely looking back, he grunted, "Keep up."

To Ezzy, it felt like an endless hike at a furious pace. In reality, it had only been about twenty-five minutes over which time they had crossed a rocky ridge and gone around a small pond. They then arrived at a wide, packed dirt trail where a strange looking sled sat harnessed to a team of slumbering Greenland dogs. Instead of runners for snow and ice, each side was outfitted with three, foot-wide, all-terrain tires.

As soon as the dogs recognized Malik, they eagerly jumped up, began howling, and pulled at their restraints.

"Whoa," said Luke to Malik. "This is your ride?"

"Yup," he replied proudly. "It's also your ride. You guys sit up front and whatever you do, don't fall off."

"Gee, thanks," muttered Ezzy as she and Luke walked to the sled, trying to figure where they were supposed to sit and how to get on. Nearing one of the dogs, Luke reached out to pet it.

"Don't!" barked Malik. "They're not pets. These are working dogs and we don't baby them like your animals at home."

Ezzy glared at the older boy. "He didn't know. Chill."

"Just get on."

"We're trying to," Ezzy snapped back. "But we've never been on a dog sled before."

Malik huffed before showing them how to get on and where to sit, one in front of the other, with their legs out straight. "There's a blanket in case you two kiddies get chilly."

Ezzy wanted to use the blanket but didn't want to give Malik the satisfaction. "We'll be fine."

Once they were situated on the sled, Malik went to the back. He picked up the reins and a whip.

Luke and Ezzy watched from up front.

"You're going to *hit* the dogs?" Luke questioned.

"No dummy, it's the sound of the whip cracking that guides them. We never actually hit them."

"Phew," Luke sighed.

The dogs strained on their harnesses, eager to run.

"When I release the brake, be ready. These guys are gonna take off. They love to run. It's what they live for."

Ezzy and Luke held tight onto the sides of the sled. Malik stepped on a lever that released the brake and quickly hopped on the back. Simultaneously, as if shot from a cannon, the dog team bolted. The sled went from a standstill to high-speed express in an instant.

Malik yelled a command and the dogs ran harder. The oldest dog was in the lead. He had thick tan fur and muscled haunches like the others, but across his back lay a distinct triangle of black. Having trained with Malik since they were puppies, the dogs followed his every command. When he yelled "iu" and cracked the whip to the right, they went left. When he yelled "ili" and cracked the whip on the other side, they went right. The boy and the dogs worked seamlessly as a team as the sled raced over the ground.

Ezzy could feel the sheer power of the dogs and was amazed at how easily Malik controlled them. She looked back and could swear he was smiling. In full command of the team, for once the boy appeared almost happy.

Ahead of her, Luke grinned, but Ezzy wasn't sure whether it was a joyous smile or a grimace due to oncoming frostbite. She buried her nose in her scarf and wrapped one arm tightly around Luke. The sled flew over the trail. But it wasn't exactly a smooth ride, and at every bump Ezzy prayed they wouldn't be catapulted out of the sled. It was frightening and at the same time exhilarating.

In surprisingly little time they covered a distance that would have taken more than an hour of hiking. The team slowed, and Ezzy recognized where they were headed.

Malik shouted and the dogs came to a halt. The team stood still, at the ready. Each dog kept glancing back as if waiting for Malik to say he didn't mean it and they should run on. The lead dog eventually sat on its haunches and the others followed. Malik set the brake, hopped off the sled, and came around to where Ezzy and Luke still sat.

"That was *so* cool," Luke told him.

Ezzy waited to see how Malik would respond to Luke's admiration. But the genuine smile she'd witnessed on the sled ride had already been replaced with his usual—a condescending sneer.

"Are you two going to sit there all day or what?" Malik said before commanding the dogs to lie down. He then strode to a door leading into the nearby, partially completed building.

Ezzy got herself and Luke up from the sled, all the while wondering why Malik was taking them into the construction site. "Why are we going in here? Isn't my dad at the hotel across the street?"

"Short cut," Malik responded. He punched a code into a lock, opened the door, and before going in turned back and added, "Coming?"

* * *

It's Easy in the Movies

Malik had disappeared into the building's dark interior. Ezzy hesitated, but Luke shrugged and followed the older boy in.

Ezzy remained behind, feeling conflicted. She assumed her father was across the street in the hotel and didn't understand why they were going into the unfinished building. And she didn't like Malik or trust him. Her gut was telling her something wasn't right, and they shouldn't follow him into the building. But Ezzy didn't fully trust her intuition, especially after last summer. She strained to see over the hillside to the road and the Arctic Palace. Taking a deep breath and trying to shrug off her unease, she then followed Luke and Malik inside.

The interior was lit by light bulbs hanging from a

wire strung along the wall. Malik and Luke were waiting inside a little way down a corridor. Its floor and walls were bare concrete. Without a word, Malik led them down the hallway to a small, square and unfurnished room. Here, the walls were painted a creamy off-white color.

Luke pointed to two shiny silver doors. "An elevator?"

"A lot of the new spa is going to be underground," Malik told them. "It's too cold most of the time for you tourists, especially in the winter. This way you can all stay comfy warm in a tunnel going from the hotel to the fancy new spa. It's also because they're tapping into the geothermal heat for the sauna and baths. It's gonna be the first of its kind here, even using new technology." He pushed the button beside the elevator doors. It glowed green.

Seconds later, a ding rang out and the doors slid open. Once inside, Ezzy noted how different it was from the unfinished part of the building. The elevator was all coziness and warmth, outfitted in dark wood with a rich rose-colored marble floor and an eye-level, flat screen showing a fire accompanied by the crackling sounds of wood burning.

"That's a bit much," Ezzy said, nodding to the virtual flames.

Malik shrugged and punched the down button. The elevator silently dropped several floors before coming to a stop. The doors slid open to a richly furnished waiting area. Dark wood chairs sported rose satin cushions. The walls were painted the same rich cream color as the room above. Several dark green stone sculptures sat on pedestals or in alcoves in the walls, all expertly highlighted by miniscule spotlights.

"Which way to the hotel?" Ezzy asked.

Malik responded by heading down a passageway to the right, clearly expecting them to follow. Ezzy noted several doors as she and Luke jogged to keep up. Malik stopped at a door on the right and opened it. He gestured for Ezzy and Luke to go inside. Luke stepped in, but Ezzy hesitated. Her spidey-sense was tingling. Something definitely didn't feel right. Before she could object, Malik shoved her from behind. She tumbled into Luke and the room as the door slammed behind them.

"Hey!" shouted Ezzy as she untangled herself from her brother. She rose and tried the door. Locked. "Let us out of here!"

"Malik!" Luke yelled.

Ezzy pounded on the door. "Malik, let us out!"

"Let us out!" Luke repeated.

Ezzy shook her head, kicking herself for not trusting her gut.

"What's going on?" Luke asked. "Why'd he lock us in?"

From outside they heard Malik talking. Each put an ear to the door to listen. "They were in the shack. They climbed out of the fjord. Must have been a rock slide below the cliff. They said they saw a pipe with steam coming off it. Yeah, yeah, I know. I explained that it's for bringing water up to the shack."

It was quiet for bit and then he added, "Yeah, nosy little boogers."

"He must be on the phone," Ezzy whispered and then put her finger to her lips to keep Luke quiet so she could hear what else Malik would say.

"Okay. Yeah, I can do that. Do you still want me to go to the new hut further up the fjord? And what about these two?"

Ezzy pushed her ear harder against the door, straining to hear.

"Okay, I'll do that when I get back."

Malik then struck the door and shouted, "Don't go anywhere. I'll be back in a bit."

"Malik! You let us out of here!" shouted Ezzy.

"It's for your own good. See ya."

Luke stared at Ezzy. "Why'd he lock us in?"

"Don't know."

"What's going on?"

"Don't know that either. But he said something about us seeing the pipe and another hut."

"Who do you think he was talking to?"

Ezzy shook her head and looked around. Light filtering in through the crack at the base of the door was enough to make out their surroundings. They were locked in a room about the size of a large walk-in closet or freezer. A table slightly bigger than the average adult lay at the center of the room, and against one wall were a cabinet, counter top, sink, and a few bare shelves. Ezzy and Luke searched the cabinet. It was empty.

Luke pounded again on the door and yelled for help. Ezzy didn't think there was anyone around to hear him. She jumped up and sat on the table then lay back thinking: *What's going on?* Who had Malik been talking to? Anguk? Were they in on it together? Was it some sort of father/son phone smuggling or steal-and-sell scheme? What was all that about the pipe and another hut?

Ezzy eventually decided it would be more productive to focus on finding a way out of the room. She'd worry about what Malik was up to later. She stared at the ceiling and smiled. "Maybe Malik isn't as smart as he thinks."

Luke gazed upward as well. "You think we'll fit?"

"They do it all the time in the movies," Ezzy told him as she stood on the table, thankful Malik had locked them in what she figured was going to be a room for massages, hence the table. Her fingertips barely reached, but she was able to jiggle the slotted vent cover directly above the table. "It's probably for air since we're underground." She worked her fingertips around the edges and pulled. "It's screwed on."

Luke smiled. "Remember what Dad gave me for my birthday, so I could always be prepared like him."

"Did you bring it with you?"

"Yup." Luke pulled a miniature multi-tool from his pocket. He opened the small screwdriver and passed it up to Ezzy.

Balancing precariously on her tiptoes, Ezzy worked on the two small screws holding the vent cover in place. Once they were loose, the screws fell out and the cover dropped. Ezzy ducked to avoid getting hit. It bounced off Luke's head. "Ouch."

"Sorry," Ezzy muttered as she reached up into the ventilation shaft to feel for the sides. But she wasn't quite tall enough. Ezzy looked around for something else to stand on, on top of the table. Not seeing anything, she turned to Luke. "I can't reach."

"I know," Luke said. "We can do the human pyramid thing like in gym. I'll get on the table and you step on me."

"That might work," Ezzy said, helping Luke up onto the table.

He got on his hands and knees and Ezzy put one foot on his back. "Tell me if I'm too heavy."

"Oomph," Luke groaned as she climbed up, adding, "I'm ... ugh... stronger than I look."

Standing on Luke, Ezzy was now high enough to pop her head up into the metal ventilation duct. It was connected to a horizontal shaft that extended in two directions. In the distance, squares of dim light periodically filtered up into the rectangular metal shaft. Reaching over her head, she put her hands and forearms up and over the edges of the shaft. "Get ready, I'm gonna push off and see if I can pull myself up."

Luke braced himself. "Ready."

Ezzy pushed off Luke's back, jumping up so that her forearms were now braced on the edges of the air shaft. Her legs dangled below. "If I can just pull myself up," she wheezed.

Ezzy curled her legs up under her and placed her feet inside the shaft. Now she was sort hanging with just her butt sticking out. "Uh oh."

"Are you stuck?" Luke asked, snickering.

"It's not funny," Ezzy told him.

"It's a little funny, sis."

Ezzy scooted her feet in further and then wiggled her butt upward. "They make it look so easy in the movies."

A muffled giggle came from below.

"I've almost got it," Ezzy groaned. "There!" She was in the air shaft, scooting back on her bottom. Then, like a circus contortionist, she turned around in the tight space and lay flat on her stomach. "Made it," she said, staring down at Luke and adding, "I think we can crawl through, and I bet it goes to the hotel."

Ezzy leaned as far over the edge of the shaft as she dared and extended one arm down. "See if you can reach my hand?"

Luke stood on the table. He reached up and Ezzy grabbed his wrist. "Remember last summer when we did the Galápagos handshake?"

Luke nodded and grabbed onto her so they were wrist-to-wrist in a solid grip. Ezzy then used her feet and other arm to help her wiggle backward in the air shaft. Luke's feet swung off the table.

"Stop swinging. It's making it harder."

"I can't help it," Luke replied. "Hurry up, feels like my hand is slipping."

Ezzy moved as quickly as she could but it was hard. And her shoulder felt like it was about to dislocate. "Hang on," she urged. "Almost there."

As soon as Luke was high enough, he reached into the vent with his other hand and helped by pulling himself up. Ezzy scooted back some more. Soon, they were both crammed inside the air shaft. Ezzy let go of Luke's wrist and lay flat, breathing hard. Luke got onto his hands and knees and looked around. "Which way?"

Ezzy pointed in the direction she hoped would lead to the hotel. "That way, I think."

Luke peered down into the room. "Maybe we should have put the cover back on. When Malik comes back, he'll know where we went."

Ezzy shrugged. "Too late now. Let's get moving."

In the distance a square of dim light filtered up into the ventilation shaft. They crawled toward it. It was another vent opening. Luke looked down and whispered, "It's another room."

"Keep going," Ezzy urged.

They crawled over the opening and continued on. Coming to a junction where the shaft intersected with another, Luke leaned forward and asked, "Which way?"

Hoping she was correct, Ezzy pointed again to the right.

As Luke crawled, he turned back to look at Ezzy. "Kinda reminds me of the tortoise tunnels last summer."

"Yeah, at least this time we're not crawling over giant turds."

From somewhere ahead, Ezzy heard faint voices. She grabbed Luke's foot and stopped. When he looked back, she put a finger to her lips.

Staying as quiet as possible, Luke and Ezzy crawled toward the sounds. Some twenty feet ahead, bright light filtered upward into the ventilation shaft. They crawled to the edge of a vent leading to another room below. Ezzy carefully lay on her stomach and peered through the slots of the cover. The only thing in view was the top of a long table made of polished blond wood. A man, presumably sitting nearby, was speaking. "Our investors are interested in the plans for the hotel and iceberg to water concept. But we need to see concrete numbers on the increase in visitors you are suggesting."

"And a demonstration with regard to the icebergs," added a woman.

Another voice answered, "I assure you the number of visitors is on the rise and will keep rising. Climate change is not slowing down, if anything it is speeding up. And with that, more and more people will want to come here to see it first-hand. Our glacier is continually in the news as the fastest melting glacier in the world. This is and will be the place to go."

"But my understanding of the science," the man from before said. "Is that melting can vary over time from year to year." He said more quietly as if to someone beside him, "I did my homework."

"Gentlemen and ladies, the scientists have been studying the glacier here for years now, and it is very clear what is happening. It is melting faster and shows no signs of slowing down. If you'd like, I can provide you with the most recent data and report from the research teams."

"But how do you know that won't change?" a woman remarked.

"Believe me, I know," the person answered. "You have my personal guarantee. Besides, recently the scientists discovered that warm ocean water is coming into the fjord, melting the ice shelf from below. They call it submarine melting. With melting of the ice shelf, the glacier behind will flow even faster to the sea and melt more."

Listening to the conversation, Ezzy suddenly had a wild idea. Make that a totally absurd idea, verging on ridiculous. It was about the pipe and steam they'd seen. Then, she heard the sound of chairs scraping on the floor below.

"With your personal guarantee, and if you can send us the data, I think we can convince our investment group to provide the cash you need. Maybe even consider a franchise. As for the iceberg to water concept, come up with a demonstration project and we'll consider that as well."

Ezzy heard a door open and the people below moving around. At the same time, a strange scent wafted up through the vent. At first it was faint, but as the people below moved about, stirring the air, it grew stronger. Ezzy's eyes grew wide in realization. She turned to Luke to tell him who was below and about her pretty bonkers idea. But before she could get the words out, her nose began to tickle. She held her breath to stop what was coming. It was no use. She sneezed. Reverberating inside the air shaft, it sounded like a minor explosion.

Down below the shuffling stopped, and someone asked, "What was that?"

There was a pause and then a woman replied, "Oh probably just something to do with the construction. No worries. Head back to your rooms and relax. I'll see you at dinner later. This is all very exciting, but I need to take care of a few things here."

As they departed, the people below thanked the woman. Ezzy heard the door shut. She and Luke hadn't moved since her sneeze.

After a quiet pause, a strong and angry voice came from below, "I know someone's up there. You better come down right this minute!"

Ezzy didn't hesitate. She pushed Luke. "Go!"

He looked back at her briefly in confusion, but then nodded and the two of them scrambled along the shaft away from the room.

Ezzy could hear someone trying to pry off the vent cover they'd just been looking through. "Faster!" she urged.

Luke looked back while continuing to crawl ahead. "I'm going as fast as I can," he said. "Who was that anyway? What's going on?"

"Didn't you recognize that god awful perfume?"

"Uh uh," Luke squeaked.

"It was Hendrik's wife, SL."

From behind them, SL said loudly, but in an overly sweet tone. "I can see you kids. That's a very dangerous place to be. You have to come out. Everyone is so worried about you. I don't know how you got in there or why, but you need to stop and come down. I can take you to your father."

Luke and Ezzy kept crawling. Ezzy heard the door in the room slam. They had to find a way out of the ventilation shaft and find their father.

Luke stopped to catch his breath. Turning to Ezzy, he asked, "What's going on, sis?"

"I can't believe you haven't figured it out Mr. Smarty-pants."

"Figured what out?"

"I think they're melting the glacier to get money for the hotel."

* * *

Rats in the Ventilation

zzy and Luke crawled as fast as they could through the ventilation shaft, searching for a way out. Along the way, Ezzy explained what she thought was going on: how SL was working with Malik and Anguk and probably Hendrik too, to melt the ice faster to attract tourists so they could get money to expand the hotel and build a spa. That's why the pipe was hot. They're pumping hot water into the fjord.

As they approached another intersection, the familiar ding of an elevator door opening rang out. Ezzy and Luke stopped and peered down through another slotted vent cover.

"There you are," a man said, though they couldn't see him.

Ezzy recognized the voice.

"Just headed back," a woman replied.

Ezzy and Luke stared at one another and whispered, "SL."

"The meeting went exceptionally well," she added. "I think we're going to get everything we need and deserve."

"Yeah," Ezzy whispered to Luke. "I sure hope so."

"That's fantastic, honey," Hendrik responded. "Your plan is working perfectly."

Ezzy had hoped that Hendrik wasn't actually part of SL's whackadoodle scheme. He seemed so nice. But his statement pretty much confirmed it. He was in on it. Together they were pumping hot water into the fjord to melt the ice shelf and cause the glacier to move and melt faster to attract crowds and impress their potential investors.

"Let's go check with the chef to be sure dinner will be unforgettable as well," Hendrik said to his wife.

"Uh," SL hesitated. "You go ahead. There's something I need to finish up with down here. Something may have gotten into the ventilation shafts, possibly some rather large rats."

"Oh darling," Hendrik replied. "Don't be silly. We can get Anguk or Malik to do that. That's no job for you."

They're definitely all in on it together, thought Ezzy. A pungent perfume-tainted mist wafted up into the air shaft. Ezzy's nose began to tickle. She pinched it trying to prevent the inevitable.

"C'mon," Hendrik said more forcefully. "If there are rats in the ventilation, they're not going anywhere anytime soon."

Ezzy squeezed her nose and held her breath.

"Okay," SL relented, adding more loudly, "I'll have someone else take care of it. Because if it is rats, they'll learn we don't like uninvited guests getting into our business."

Ezzy couldn't hold it in any longer. She sneezed just as the elevator doors closed.

"That was close," Luke noted.

Ezzy nodded. "C'mon, let's get out of here." She positioned herself over the vent cover below, adding, "Here goes nothing." She kicked the slotted metal square with both feet as hard as she could. It bent but didn't come loose.

"Try again," Luke encouraged.

Ezzy bent up her legs and again kicked the thin metal cover. This time it broke loose and clattered on the floor.

"You go first," Ezzy told her brother.

They did the Galápagos wrist-to-wrist grip again and Ezzy lowered Luke as far as she could. It was still about a three-foot drop to the floor.

"Ready?" Ezzy asked. "On three. One... two... three!"

Luke fell to the floor and rolled onto his side before climbing to his feet.

"You okay?"

"Yup, your turn."

Ezzy turned backward so that her legs hung down from the air shaft. She lowered herself as best she could until she was hanging from her hands. It wasn't a long drop, but still she hesitated.

"Let go," Luke urged.

"I know," Ezzy snapped. Her hands began to slip. She let go. Landing, she bent her knees to absorb the impact.

Luke was about to push the button for the elevator when Ezzy grabbed his hand. "Wait. They might still be up there. Maybe there are stairs."

Ezzy ran down the connecting corridor to the right to look for a stairway. She was glad to leave the luxuriously decorated waiting area outside the elevators. It still smelled like SL.

Luke had gone to the left and soon shouted back, but not too loudly. "Over here!"

Ezzy sprinted to him. Luke held the door open and they peered into the stairwell. It was empty. Cautiously, they began climbing the stairs.

"We need to find Dad and tell him what happened," Ezzy said. "And about what they're doing."

"Do you really think they're pumping hot water into the fjord to melt the ice faster?"

"Yes."

Three flights up they came to a door. Ezzy put her ear against it.

"Hear anything?" Luke asked.

"Na uh." Ezzy slowly turned the knob and opened the door a crack to look out. "I think we're near the place where people check in."

"Do you see anyone?"

"No, coast looks clear. C'mon and act casual. We'll head to the room. That's probably where Dad is."

Ezzy grabbed Luke's hand as they nervously stepped out of the stairway into the hotel lobby.

"There you are!" someone exclaimed.

Ezzy turned. It was Hendrik, the owner of the Arctic Palace, and right beside him was SL along with a small group of new guests checking in.

"We've all been so worried about you two," he said.

Yeah, right, Ezzy thought.

"Where have you been?" Hendrik added.

"Yes, and your father has been so very worried," SL remarked. "We were all worried."

"Uh," stammered Ezzy, not sure how to respond or what to say. All the people in the lobby had stopped what they were doing and now stared at her and Luke as if they were number one on the FBI's most wanted list.

"Are you okay?" Hendrik asked.

"We're fine," Ezzy answered. "Where's our dad?"

"Come with me and let's get him," he answered.

Before Ezzy could scream, run or react in any way, the man grabbed Luke's hand and pulled him down the corridor. As her brother was dragged away, he turned back to Ezzy and mouthed—help me.

"Let go of him!" Ezzy yelled.

Without even a look back, Hendrik, along with Luke, disappeared through a nearby doorway.

Ezzy sprinted after them, while SL smiled at the guests checking in. "Kids these days."

SL then strolled casually after Ezzy and followed her through the doorway. She pointedly closed the door as she went in.

Ezzy had nearly bowled Luke over when she ran into the room. The two now stood watching Hendrik. The man was behind a large desk facing them with his hands on his hips and a dour expression on his face. He shook his head at them before punching a number into a phone on the desk. He raised the phone and spoke softly into it.

"What... what are you going to do to us?" Ezzy asked.

"Do to you?" Hendrik responded.

Seconds later, the door to the office flew open and Dr. Skylar rushed in. As soon as he saw Ezzy and Luke, he ran to them and pulled them into his arms. "Thank god. I was so worried. Are you okay?"

Being held in a tight hug, Ezzy and Luke's responses were muffled.

"Don't ever do that again."

Luke pulled back from his father. "Do what? It's not like it was our fault or anything."

Ezzy stepped back as well. "Yeah, Dad. Believe me, we didn't go traipsing across the ice for the fun of it."

"Well then," he replied. "What exactly happened, and how did you get here?"

Ezzy glanced at SL before saying, "We're really tired. Can we go back to the room and talk about it there?"

"We'd like to hear as well," Hendrik told them.

"Yes, very much," added his wife.

"Why don't you have a seat," Hendrik suggested, pointing to a sitting area in one corner of the room. "I'll have some warm beverages brought in." He placed an order through the phone, while Dr. Skylar encouraged Ezzy and Luke to sit down.

Moments later a restaurant waiter arrived and passed around steaming cups of coffee and hot cocoa.

"Now," Hendrik said. "I sent Anguk to pick you up and bring you back as your father requested."

Dr. Skylar interjected, "I decided I wasn't so comfortable with you two being out there on your own and had arranged for a private whale watching tour for just the three of us."

Hendrik then continued, "But Anguk says that the boat ran aground on the ice due to some whales bubble-feeding—which is quite remarkable, by the way. And then you two hopped out and ran away. Why in the world did you do that?"

"Yes, why in the world?" repeated their father.

Ezzy was about to answer, but Luke jumped in excitedly, "That guy Anguk had a gun and wanted Ezzy's phone. He said he wanted to take our picture, but he really wanted to steal it. Then a whale swallowed it. Then he fell and hit his head. We had nothing to do with it. But he looked at us like it was our fault and kept looking at the gun. That's why we got out of the boat. And then—"

Hendrik held up his hand. "Hold on. Are you saying Anguk threatened you and tried to steal your phone?"

"Yes," Ezzy replied.

Hendrik shook his head. "I've known Anguk for years. He would absolutely never threaten a guest or steal. He's worked here since we opened. He always has the rifle in case of polar bears and for hunting seals. I'm sure he meant no harm. I told him to give you two a little tour of the icebergs on the way back and take some photos."

"That's not what it seemed like," Ezzy said and Luke nodded.

"You must have misunderstood the situation," Hendrik told them.

"I'd like to speak with him," Dr. Skylar said to Hendrik.

"Of course, but he was the one that reported them missing. Came back as soon as he could to help."

"What happened after that?" their father asked.

Ezzy and Luke then recounted their trek across the icefjord. Whenever Luke began to describe something that sounded especially perilous or life threatening, Ezzy cut in to make it sound less dangerous so that her dad wouldn't be so upset with them. After a pointed look, Luke caught on and together they tried to tone down the drama of their near-death experience. When they got to the part about finding the shack and climbing out of the fjord, Ezzy purposely left out the steam and pipe they'd spotted.

"It was fortunate that you found the science shack," Hendrik remarked.

"Yup," Ezzy muttered.

"Yeah, and then Malik showed up and gave us a ride back on his dog sled," Luke added. "That part was cool."

"How come you didn't come right back to the hotel?" their father asked.

Ezzy stared directly at SL. "Because Malik locked us in a room in the new spa building."

"What?" Dr. Skylar asked.

"Hold on," said SL. "I think this is just another misunderstanding, like with Anguk."

Ezzy glared as the woman continued, "Malik was worried you'd run off again and wanted to keep you safe. It might not have been the smartest thing to have done, but it was to keep you two secure. He called me right after and I went to get you, but you'd already climbed up into the ventilation shaft."

"What?" Dr. Skylar repeated.

"Well, Dad," Ezzy snapped. "He locked us in!"

"And we heard him talking on the phone," Luke added. "He was going to come back and do something to us."

"He was probably talking to me," SL noted. "But I was just asking him where you were so I could come get you as quickly as possible. He had to leave to finish some chores. Again, I think you two misunderstood or have very active imaginations."

Too angry now to hold back, Ezzy shouted, "No! We did not misunderstand. We know what we saw and heard."

"What do you mean?" her father asked.

Ezzy gritted her teeth, turned to Luke and nodded before saying, "They're melting the ice so some guys will give them money for the hotel."

"Who's melting, what ice?" her father asked.

Ezzy pointed to Hendrik and his wife. "Them."

"What?" Hendrik exclaimed. "That's ridiculous. We are doing no such thing."

"That is an outrageous accusation, young lady," SL added.

"She's telling the truth," Luke said. "We saw a pipe going down into the fjord from the shack and it was hot. And then we heard them talking about it."

Hendrik chuckled and shook his head. "You two have definitely been watching too many movies. That's just a pipe to bring water up into the shack."

"Then why was it hot?" Ezzy asked.

"I'm sure it just appeared that way," SL offered, shaking her head. "Like fog or mist, something to do with the surrounding cold air. You two probably had a bit of hypothermia and must have been traumatized by that awful experience on the icebergs. And besides, I can assure you, the glacier and ice shelf are melting all on their own. We have nothing to do with it."

Ezzy glared at the woman. "We heard you telling those people you could guarantee the ice would melt faster."

"Yes," SL responded. "Because that is what the researchers are finding. Nothing more. My, you really do have a wild imagination."

Ezzy wanted to scream. SL and Hendrik were lying. How could her father not believe her?

"Clearly, there has been some sort of colossal misunderstanding here. A series of misunderstandings, really," Dr. Skylar announced and then turned to his kids.

"We will be having a serious discussion about decision-making and consequences. Though the important thing is that you two are back safe and sound and no one was hurt. C'mon, let's go back to the room and get you cleaned up."

"But, Dad," Ezzy said.

"Enough," her father told her and then turned to Hendrik and his wife. "I'm so sorry for the confusion and trouble."

"No worries. Just as you said, a giant misunderstanding," SL responded. "And you two kids must be starving. We'll have some food sent to the room."

Now she's acting all nice, Ezzy thought.

"I'd still like to speak with Anguk," Dr. Skylar told them. "And I hope you'll talk to Malik. Clearly, locking my kids in a room was both unnecessary and frightening for them."

"Of course," Hendrik replied.

Dr. Skylar thanked Hendrik and SL for all their efforts to find his kids and again apologized for all the trouble they caused. He then led Ezzy and Luke out of the office. They walked in silence to their room. As soon as the door closed, their father sat down on the sofa and said, "Okay, hot showers for you both and then I want to hear exactly what happened out there. Everything in painstaking detail."

Heading toward their room, Ezzy turned back. "Dad, I know what we saw and heard. They're lying."

"Get warm, clean up, and we'll talk about it."

Ezzy nodded. Luke had gone into their bathroom, so she grabbed her pajamas and headed for her dad's shower. All the while she couldn't help but think about what had happened. She was sure about SL and the pipe, but was less certain about Katya's father. Did it just seem like he was trying to steal her phone and threaten them? Was he really just showing them the icebergs and trying to take photos? She guessed it was possible. He'd never been a friendly sort of guy. But if she was wrong about him, then she'd put Luke in terrible danger crossing the ice. She'd feel terrible if that was true. Then she thought about Malik. Could he have locked them in the room for their own safety? She found that hard to believe, especially since SL suggested it. What about Hendrik? What was his role in all of this?

* * *

Less Drama, More Proof

After a long, hot, much-needed shower, Ezzy joined Luke and her father in the sitting area outside their bedrooms. Room service had delivered a stack of hamburgers and a precariously tall tower of French fries. Luke was already halfway through a burger by the time Ezzy sat down.

"So much for giving up real burgers," Ezzy said to her brother.

With his mouth full, Luke grinned. "Hey, I am so hungry right now, I'd eat just about anything." Then he shrugged. "Well, almost anything. Still not eating seals or whales."

"Right there with you pal. Pass one of those burgers over here."

"So," their father began. "Luke here has been telling me more about what happened on the boat and ice."

Luke simply nodded to Ezzy.

"But Ez," her father continued. "I'd like to hear it from you also."

In between bites, Ezzy explained what happened starting from when Anguk came to pick them up in the small boat. She still held back some of the more scary and dangerous parts of their ordeal, thinking if her father knew too much it would make the whole situation worse. He asked a few questions as Luke watched intently.

After she'd told him *almost* everything, Ezzy paused and waited nervously to see what her dad would say. Would he believe her and feel bad or concerned, or was she in a big pot of doo-doo? Her father sat in silent contemplation for a few minutes before speaking.

"I fully believe what you two *think* you saw and heard. And certainly, that boy, Malik, should not have locked you in that room."

Ezzy felt a momentary wave of relief, but the look on her father's face suggested she wasn't totally out of the crap pile yet.

"But, and that is a big but, I have to question your assessment of Anguk's actions and the rash decision to run away across the ice. That was very dangerous and you both could have been seriously hurt or even killed."

"But Dad," Ezzy began.

Her father held up his hand. "Let me finish. Some people are socially awkward and come across as unpleasant or difficult, that doesn't mean they are dangerous or would hurt you. I've had a little interaction with Anguk, and I have to say I agree with Hendrik and think you misjudged him. He's not what I'd call a people-person. Maybe you were a little rash in how you judged him because of what happened last summer. If anything, I blame myself. I should not have allowed you to go on that boat ride without me."

Ezzy's immediate reaction was to disagree and fight back. But before she said anything, she stopped and took a big breath. She again thought back to what had happened. "*Maybe* we *were* wrong about Katya's father. But it really did seem at the time like he was threatening us and wanted the phone."

"I understand that," her dad replied.

"It did," Luke added.

Ezzy turned to her brother. "I... I'm sorry. If I was wrong that means we should never have gotten out of the boat and run across the ice."

"It's not your fault," Luke told her. "I was scared of him too. Besides, you saved me on the iceberg."

Ezzy nodded and then turned to her father. "I might have screwed up there, Dad. I'm really sorry."

"From now on, I want you to think carefully before you act, especially so rashly."

"I will, Dad. I swear. But what about that pipe and

what we heard SL say to those investor people? I don't think we were wrong about that. And I still don't buy that Malik locked us in the room for our safety. That's just stupid."

"You know, on that we agree," her father replied. "Malik was wrong to do that. You two crawling into the air shaft was pretty daring and clever, but again very dangerous. As for Mr. and Mrs. Rise being behind some wild scheme to melt the ice faster to gain investment, well, that seems pretty farfetched. Again, maybe the experience last summer has made you more suspicious of people and quick to judge their actions as nefarious. Like she said, SL could have been referring to what the science teams are already finding at the glacier."

"But Dad," said Luke. "The pipe going into the fjord really was hot."

"Yeah," said Ezzy. "And steaming. I swear."

"Could it have been fog or mist associated with the cold air like SL suggested?"

Luke shrugged as if it was a possibility.

Ezzy shook her head with confidence. "No Dad. Our hands were freezing, so we held them over the pipe to warm up. It was hot. I'm sure of it."

Luke now nodded. "Yeah, that's right."

"Well, that I can't explain," Dr. Skylar told them. "But I find it extremely hard to believe they are actually pumping warm water into the fjord for money."

Ezzy huffed in frustration. "Dad, I'm right about this."

Luke again nodded. "*We're* right about this."

"What if we could prove it?" Ezzy added.

"How?" asked her father.

"Let's go back to the shack and we'll show you."

Dr. Skylar stared thoughtfully at his kids. "Well, we do have a few more days here. And I would love to see more of the fjord. Where exactly is the shack? And how far is it?"

"I... *think* I can get us there," Ezzy told him.

Luke's eyes got wide. "Hey, I know someone that could help. At least show us where it is on a map or something."

"Who?" Dr. Skylar asked.

"Katya," Luke said. "She probably knows where it is."

Ezzy nodded. "Yeah, and I'm sure she's not in on the whole melt the ice for big bucks thing."

"I'll think about it," their father responded. "Let's get some sleep and we can talk about it more in the morning."

Ezzy was sure if they could show him the hot pipe, they could prove they were right about SL and Hendrik melting the glacier. It might even make up a little for her being wrong about Anguk. If she really was wrong. In the back of her mind, Ezzy wasn't completely convinced that he wasn't in on everything and hadn't wanted to steal her phone. "Really Dad, if we could go there, we could prove it."

"Yeah," Luke added.

"Sleep first," their father responded. "We'll talk more in the morning."

Ezzy and Luke went to their room. Exhausted both physically and mentally, Ezzy crawled into bed and snuggled under the covers. She turned to Luke to discuss how best in the morning to convince their father to go to the science shack. But his eyes were closed and from his mouth came soft murmurs almost like a cat purring. Luke was already deep in dreamland.

* * *

Poop, Puppies, and a Plan

E zzy woke up more determined than ever to prove that she and Luke were right about the hot pipe and the whole melt-the-glacier scheme. But she decided to wait until after breakfast to say anything. Luke, however, beat her to it. While chomping on a banana-nut muffin, he turned eagerly to their father. "Dad, can we go back to the science shack to show you the pipe and everything? Can we?"

"Please," added Ezzy.

"How about we start by seeing if your friend Katya can point it out on the map of the hiking trails?"

Luke nodded.

"Sounds good," said Ezzy, trying to be as agreeable and helpful as possible. "You know, Dad, if you want to rest or something, Luke and I can find Katya and ask about the location of the shack. You don't really need to come."

"Ezmeralda," her father responded. "For the rest of this trip, I am not letting either one of you out of my sight."

Given their recent exploits on the ice and in the ventilation shaft, Ezzy wasn't surprised by her father's reaction. But she hoped it didn't mean that he had suddenly turned into one of those helicopter parents that constantly hovers around his or her kids. She liked the fact that he gave them freedom and encouraged them to do things on their own. Her mother had always pushed the importance of independence and being self-sufficient.

They finished breakfast and headed toward the puppy enclosure, where they hoped to find Katya. When they arrived, Ezzy was glad to find the young girl there, but not so happy that she wasn't alone. Holding a shovel and skulking nearby in the pen, was Malik. As they approached, he looked up, put the shovel down, and headed their way.

Uh oh, thought Ezzy.

"I'm supposed to apologize," said Malik, glaring at Ezzy and Luke.

It wasn't what Ezzy expected him to say and she couldn't resist milking it a bit. "What was that?"

Malik grimaced. "You're going to make this hard, aren't you?"

Ezzy shrugged as Katya stared pointedly at Malik.

"Remember, I did rescue you from the shack."

"Apologize," Katya urged.

"Yeah, well. I'm very sorry I locked you in the room." Malik paused before adding, "Like SL said, I was just trying to help. Keeping you safe and all that. You shouldn't have climbed out of there."

Ezzy stared at the boy. She thought his apology sounded about as fake as the excuse he gave for locking them in the room.

Dr. Skylar stepped forward and reached out a hand. "Thank you, young man. It takes a lot to admit our mistakes and it is important to learn from them." He shook the boy's hand and then turned to Ezzy and Luke.

"What?" Ezzy said.

"You need to accept his apology."

"I accept your apology," Ezzy announced, muttering under her breath, "not."

Luke nodded. "And the sled ride was pretty awesome."

Malik then turned to his sister. "Was that good enough? Do I have to shovel any more dog crap?"

The girl snickered. "Dad said you had to apologize and clean out the entire pen."

Malik grumbled, turned his back on the group, and strode angrily to the far side of the pen.

"I heard what happened," Katya told them. "And I'm really sorry about what Malik did."

"Thanks," Luke replied. "Where are the puppies?"

"They're locked in the doghouse while we clean out here. We can go see them if you want."

Luke again nodded.

"But," Katya added. "I just want to say my dad isn't the most friendly or social person, especially since my mom left. But he would never hurt you."

Ezzy stared at her feet and fidgeted nervously. "Yeah, I guess... I guess I might have been wrong about that. I'm sorry too."

"We both are," Luke told the girl.

"Don't get me wrong," Katya added. "He can come across as sorta mean, especially to visitors. It's because of what happened."

"What do you mean?" Ezzy asked.

Katya frowned. "My mom left us to go live with some guy she met at the hotel. Ever since, my dad and Malik aren't all that nice to guests."

"Oh dear," Dr. Skylar responded. "I can understand how that might make them and you feel. I'm so sorry."

"Me too," Luke said.

"It was a while ago," Katya told them.

"Do you still see her? Your mom?" Luke asked.

Katya shook her head sadly. "No. She didn't like living in Greenland. I think she wanted to live someplace easier. Everything here costs a lot and is hard to get. And the winters are kinda tough. But Dad says she still loves us. She sends us letters, and packages on our birthdays and at Christmas. I'm hoping one day maybe I can visit her."

"That must be very hard for you and your brother," noted Dr. Skylar. "But I am sure she still loves you."

Katya nodded. "Hendrik and SL have been really good to us. And SL has become almost like a mother to Malik. She's even made him her assistant around the hotel and stuff."

Ezzy didn't know what to say. An awkward silence ensued until Luke piped up, "Can we play with the puppies now?"

"Sure," Katya replied as she headed toward the doghouse. As they approached, a frenzy of excited high-pitched yipping began.

"Hey, Katya," Ezzy said, remembering why they were there. "Do you know where the science shack is? The one where Malik found us?"

"Sure," she answered as she unlatched the door to the doghouse.

Seconds later, three balls of tan fur flew out and pounced on Luke, again knocking him to the ground. He squealed with glee and giggled as the puppies climbed all over him and licked his face.

The others couldn't help but laugh.

"Can you show us where the shack is on a map?" Ezzy asked. "We want to show our dad."

"Yeah, sure" Katya replied. "Are you gonna go there?"

"Uh huh, hopefully later. Right, Dad?"

Dr. Skylar nodded.

"I'm not doing anything," Katya told them. "I could go with you if you want."

"If it's okay with your father," Dr. Skylar responded. "We'd love for you to come."

Katya turned to her brother who was slowly walking about the other side of the pen clearly on the hunt for additional piles of puppy poop. "I bet I could get my dad to make Malik give us a ride on his sled. He's supposed to be practicing. SL and Hendrik have asked him to create a new guest experience for when there's no ice—dogsled-on-wheels."

"Uh... ," started Ezzy. She didn't want Malik to go with them.

"That would be great," said Dr. Skylar. "I heard about that ride. It sounded quite exciting."

"Exciting only because we didn't die," added Ezzy.

Katya chuckled. "I can get him to go a little slower this time."

"Okay," Dr. Skylar said. "How about you ask your dad and then give us a call. We're in room 208. We thought we'd go out after lunch."

"Cool," Katya answered. "I'll ask my dad as soon as we're done here."

Katya, Ezzy, and Dr. Skylar joined Luke on the ground playing with the puppies. One of the dogs jumped on Ezzy and pulled playfully at the extra-long red scarf she'd chosen to wear that morning. It was hard to tell the puppies apart, but she thought it was Dante, the puppy she had rescued from the ditch. Out of the corner of her eye, Ezzy eyed Malik. At the far side of the pen, he now stood glowering at them.

*   *   *

Return to the Icefjord

It was mid-afternoon and Ezzy stood on the boardwalk near the unfinished spa building next to her father and Luke. The sky was a cloudless blue and the air crisp and relatively warm. She was anxious as she thought about going to the science shack and how it was probably their only shot at proving they were right about the whole hot water and melting the glacier thing. She tapped her father on the shoulder. "Do you think Malik is coming too?"

"I'm not sure," he answered. "But the boy did apologize, Ez. Let's give him a break. His life hasn't been easy."

"I don't trust him."

"Please, no more drama. Just cool your engines."

Luke snickered. "It's cool your *jets* dad."

Dr. Skylar ruffled his son's hair. "Malik said he was sorry, and besides, after what Katya told us, it's easy to understand why he and his father might act a little off with guests." He glanced toward the hotel and added, "Hey, looks like our ride is here."

As the dogsled approached, Malik shouted a command and the team slowed. He shouted again and the dogs came to an immediate stop beside the boardwalk.

"Greenland taxi at your service," said Katya, who was sitting on the front of the sled.

"Yeah, at your service," griped Malik. "Are you sure you want to go back to the shack? Not much to see there. The icebergs are much better further downstream."

"Yeah," Luke observed. "We know all about the icebergs. Thanks, but no thanks. I'm all about staying on solid ground now."

"They want to go to the science shack," Katya told Malik. "It'll be fun. Besides, you can impress them with your sledding skills." She then showed the Skylars how to get onto the front of the sled and where to sit. Once they were seated, Katya went to the back to stand beside her brother.

Dr. Skylar raised his eyebrows playfully. "Okay, everyone hang on, this is gonna be *awesome.*"

A quick shout from Malik and the dog team took off. Within seconds they were racing down a wide packed-dirt trail. Once again, Malik controlled the team with ease, ushering the sled around sharp turns and over small hills. Ezzy held on tight, having fun but also in fear for her life. Going over a ditch, the sled suddenly dipped down and then leapt up. If Ezzy hadn't grabbed onto Luke's jacket, she swore he would have flown off.

Malik brought them to a halt. "Sorry 'bout that," he mumbled. "Permafrost thaw."

"Everyone okay?" Dr. Skylar asked.

"We're cool, right Ez?" Luke replied.

She nodded and turned back to glare at Malik, wondering if he'd hit the ditch on purpose.

Seconds later, they were back up to dogsled express speed. After winding around a long wide curve, they came to a stop. Malik put on the brake. "This is as far as the dogs can go. The shack is just over the next ridge."

Ezzy glanced around. "Are you sure this is the same place? It seemed like a longer ride from the shack before?"

"It's the same, just took a slightly different route this time."

Dr. Skylar, Ezzy, and Luke climbed off the sled to follow Katya, who'd begun hiking up a gradual slope of gray rocks. Katya turned back to her brother. "Are you coming?"

"Nope. Not part of the deal. Meet you back here in like two hours. That should give you plenty of time to do whatever it is you're doing."

"Okay, but don't forget."

Malik glared at his sister and then released the brake. He shouted at the dogs, and with less weight on the sled, they took off even faster than before. Within minutes they were out of sight.

Katya led the Skylars across the rocks and through a patch of crinkly gray and orange mossy plants. At the top of the rise, the icefjord came into view along with a small wooden hut at its edge. After a short hike, they reached the shack. Luke offered to get the key while the others waited at the door.

"How'd you know where the key was?" Dr. Skylar asked.

"Dumb luck," Ezzy offered.

"More like awesome brains," Luke answered as he pulled the magnetic box from under the thermometer. He removed the key and unlocked the door.

Katya went directly to the stove and turned it on. "It's actually pretty cozy in here. Sometimes the scientists let me tag along and hang out with them. Want some hot cocoa?"

"Sure," Luke responded.

"Sounds good," his father added.

Luke and Katya prepared four cups of steaming chocolatey goodness.

"Does the water come from the fjord?" Dr. Skylar asked the girl.

"Uh huh, pumped up out back."

"That must be the pipe we saw," Luke added. "And the steam."

Katya looked confused. "Steam?"

"C'mon Dad, we'll show you," said Ezzy, chugging her drink and heading for the door.

At the edge of the cliff, Ezzy stared out over the fjord. The ice had shifted a little, but their paddle berg was still stuck in the mud below. With melting, it had gone from extra-large dining to coffee table size. Luke joined them and pointed below. "That's the iceberg we paddled to shore on."

Dr. Skylar stared out over the jumble of icebergs mashed together in the fjord. "You crossed over that?"

Ezzy winced and knowingly eyed her brother. "It was... uh... easier than it looks."

Katya had followed Luke out. "How'd you climb up?"

"Over here," Luke said, showing them a narrow zigzag cut in the rocks leading down to the beach and mud below.

"That doesn't look very safe," his father noted.

"Yeah well, compared to the ice it was a breeze," Luke responded. When he saw Ezzy staring at him and shaking her head, he added, "I mean it wasn't that bad, Dad."

"C'mon," Ezzy urged her father. "I want to show you the pipe. The one that was hot."

Katya looked at Luke curiously. "A hot pipe? What's she talking about?"

Luke ignored the girl's question and leaned over to scan the area below.

Dr. Skylar pulled him back from the edge. "Not so close."

"We need to go down there," Ezzy said. "To see it."

"Well then, only you and I will go," her father replied.

"I want to go too," Luke told him.

"I know, son, but I'd prefer if you stay up here with Katya. I was willing to come out here so you could show me this mysterious pipe, the least you can do is give me this and stay up here. Nice and safe."

"But Dad."

"No buts. Sit tight. We'll be back soon."

Ezzy began to inch her way carefully down the cliff trail.

Her father followed. "Go slow, Ez, and be careful."

"Don't worry Dad, I have no intention of cracking my head open now."

"Don't even say it."

As they descended, Ezzy glanced back at Katya who appeared to be questioning Luke. She figured the girl was probably wondering what they were looking for. Distracted by her thoughts, Ezzy stepped in a patch of slick mud. Her foot slipped and she nearly did a split. Dr. Skylar grabbed her jacket. "Gotcha."

Ezzy took a deep breath, composed herself, and continued down. She wanted to be the picture of confidence for her father, even if her heart felt like it was about to leap out of her chest. Once she reached the rock-strewn beach, Ezzy relaxed a little and led her father to the base of the cliff below the shack. She scanned the area searching for a cloud of steam like they'd seen before. Nothing. She moved closer to the cliff and climbed a little way up to where she thought the pipe should be. Tightly packed rocks covered the area. "It was right about here, Dad."

"Are you sure that's the spot?"

"Yes," answered Ezzy. "Pretty sure."

She looked around wondering if it was the right spot. There was no steam or pipe anywhere. She turned back to where she thought the pipe should be and moved closer, holding her hands over the rocks. No change in temperature. Staring at the rocks, she noticed that they looked particularly well-packed and orderly. Had it been like that before? She didn't think it had been so—so neat. She remembered it had looked like there'd been some sort of landslide that had left piles of dirt and scattered rocks around the pipe. Could someone have covered it up? She moved a few of the stones aside, but still no pipe. She began to dig into the dirt.

"Honey, it's okay. You don't need to get all dirty."

"Dad, I'm pretty sure this is the spot."

About six inches down, Ezzy felt something hard. "Here, Dad. It's right here." She shoved more dirt aside.

Her father moved closer. "It must be the pipe for water from the fjord."

Ezzy felt the pipe. It was cool to the touch. "I swear it was hot before. And there *was* steam coming off it."

Her father felt the pipe. "Well, it's definitely not hot now. C' mon Ez, cover it up and let's go back up. You were right there is a pipe here."

"But Dad, it *was* hot."

"C'mon kiddo, let's go."

Ezzy hesitated. She wasn't wrong about this. That pipe had been hot before. Maybe she'd been wrong about Anguk and her phone. She was willing to admit that and felt bad about it. But she was sure about this. She jogged after her father who was now waiting for her at the base of the cliff. They headed up the trail.

Waiting for them above, Luke leaned over and shouted, "Did you find the pipe?"

"Yes," his father yelled back.

When they reached the top, Luke turned to Ezzy. "Was it hot and steaming again?"

Ezzy shook her head.

"Weird," Luke said. "Do you think... I mean... were we wrong about it?"

Katya still appeared confused. "Wrong? Wrong about what?"

Ezzy pursed her lips. "The pipe was hot because someone is pumping hot water into the fjord to melt the glacier faster."

"What?"

"Ezzy," her father said. "Like SL suggested, you and Luke went through a very traumatic experience out on the ice. I think you were confused. It's very understandable."

"No, Dad," Ezzy said sharply. "I know what we saw and heard."

Luke stood up straighter. "She's right. We did see steam coming off the pipe and used it to warm our hands. And SL said she could guarantee the ice would melt faster."

Katya stared at them, and their father shook his head.

Ezzy clenched her fists in frustration, getting angry. "We're not making it up. And we're not wrong. Someone came up here and covered up the pipe. I know it. Probably turned off whatever was making it hot." She figured it was probably Malik but didn't want to say so in front of Katya.

"And you think it's *SL* doing that?" Katya asked.

Ezzy nodded. After an awkward silence, she added, "What if we could prove it another way?"

"What do you mean?" Dr. Skylar asked.

Ezzy turned to Luke. "Do you remember when we heard Malik talking on the phone? He said there's another shack further up the glacier."

"You're right," Luke said excitedly.

"There is," Katya noted. "It's just another science shack and weather station."

"I bet they're pumping hot water into the fjord up there too," Ezzy said. "And they don't know we know about it."

"Yeah," Luke agreed.

"C'mon, Dad, let's go up there," Ezzy urged. "I may have been wrong about Katya's father and the phone. But I... I'm not wrong about this. Let me prove it."

Dr. Skylar looked at his watch and up at the sky. "Well, I guess here we don't have to worry about it getting dark. Katya, how far is the next shack from here?"

"Not too far."

"Please Dad," Ezzy pleaded. "Let me prove I wasn't wrong about this."

"*We* weren't wrong," corrected Luke.

"Well, if it's just a short hike." He turned to Katya. "Can we make it up there and still be back in time for our ride back?"

"I can text Malik and tell him to come a little later."

"No!" shouted Ezzy. "Don't tell him we're going up there."

"Why?" Katya asked.

Luke shook his head.

Ezzy stuttered, "Er... because..."

Katya stared at her.

"Because we think Malik is involved."

"What?" Katya responded. "No way."

"He locked us in that room."

Katya frowned and shook her head. "You're wrong about him *and SL.* No way they are doing that."

"Well, then let's go to the next shack to see, one way or the other," Ezzy urged.

"We've come this far," Dr. Skylar noted. "What's another short hike?"

They went back into the shack to straighten up before leaving. Once inside, however, Ezzy noticed that Katya had hung back. She was about to go back outside to see what the girl was doing, when Katya entered the hut.

* * *

Ice Tunnels

The hike heading up to the second science shack was uneventful. Katya led them on a narrow trail over rocks, through grass, and around squishy moss. Off to their right, more icebergs drifted slowly through the fjord toward Disko Bay. After a quick stop for snacks and water, the group continued on.

Just when Ezzy was beginning to think Katya's idea of a "short" hike was misguided at best, the young girl stopped and pointed ahead. "There it is."

Not too far away sat another small green wooden hut with a weather station to the side.

"Hey! Katya!" someone shouted.

Startled, the group turned back to see Malik jogging their way. Out of breath, he stopped alongside his sister and gasped, "Where's your phone? I tried calling and texting."

Katya shrugged. "Sorry, didn't hear it. Besides, you know, this far out, a signal is pretty iffy."

Malik sucked in a big breath and shook his head. "The scientists have an experiment in the shack and don't want anyone going in there."

"What?" Katya questioned. "Are you sure? I haven't heard anything about it. Dad would have told me."

"Well, I'm telling you now."

Ezzy and Luke exchanged a skeptical glance.

"Maybe we better not go in then," Dr. Skylar announced. "Wouldn't want to mess anything up."

"Can we at least look around?" Ezzy asked.

"Yeah," Luke added.

Malik glared at them. "No, you can't. You should just go back to the hotel."

Ezzy ignored him and headed for the shack. "You can't stop us."

Malik raced after her and blocked her path. "Try me."

The others caught up and Katya stepped up to her brother. "What's gotten into you? They're just gonna look around. No big deal."

"They could mess things up."

"What things? Malik, you're acting even weirder than usual."

"C'mon, Katya. These experiments are... uh sensitive... and besides... Dad wants you home."

Katya put her hands on her hips and stared at her brother. "No, he doesn't. He said I could come out here."

Malik eyed his sister. "You need to do what I say."

"Says who?" Katya responded.

Malik exhaled loudly in frustration.

Katya continued to stare curiously at her brother.

"You're going to ruin everything," he whispered to her.

Overhearing, Ezzy asked, "Ruin what?"

Malik glanced around and then bowed his head. After a long pause, he looked up and eyed his sister as if deciding something. Then he turned to the group. "Okay, there is something going on, but I can't tell you what it is. Just believe me. It's better if you all go back to the hotel now."

Dr. Skylar stepped up to the boy. "Son, I think you'd better tell me exactly what's going on."

"I'd rather not."

"I think you'd better," the man responded.

Malik turned to Katya. "You had to be all chummy and come with them." He let out a groan of frustration. "These guys are not playing around. That scientist's accident, do you really think her rope broke on its own? They're dangerous."

"Who?" Katya asked.

"C'mon, son," Dr. Skylar said. "Maybe I can help."

Malik sighed and gazed out over the fjord. "It started about a year ago with the new spa and expanding the hotel. SL said she had investors, so Hendrik did the planning and started to build. But then, the big money guys pulled out and they'd already spent a ton. SL said that if they didn't do something to get the investors to change their minds or find new ones, they'd have to close the hotel. She said if we could draw in crowds and show that the place had bigtime financial potential, it would save the hotel and everyone's jobs."

"Go on," Dr. Skylar urged.

"Well, the researchers had already found that the glacier and ice shelf were melting and some of it was because of warm water rising up in the fjord. So she... well... decided to help it along. That way she could promote this as the fastest melting glacier in the world and it would produce even more icebergs."

"I assume *she* is SL," Dr. Skylar noted. "What exactly did she do?"

Malik hesitated. "She built the science shacks saying they were for the researchers, but secretly installed a heater and pump in the back so that warm water could be injected into the fjord."

"I knew it!" exclaimed Ezzy.

"Yeah, *we* knew it," added Luke.

Katya stared at her brother. "Did you help her?"

"Kinda," Malik replied. "I mean it's not like anyone got hurt until that researcher fell into the moulin."

Concern creased Dr. Skylar's brow. "What do you mean? I thought that was an accident."

"Some of the people helping the researchers work for SL. Hired stooges, not from around here. She doesn't want the scientists putting too much equipment under the ice and in the fjord. She's afraid they might discover what she's doing. But honest, I didn't have anything to do with tampering with their ropes."

"Does Dad know?" Katya asked tentatively.

"No, he has nothing to do with it."

"What about Hendrik?" Ezzy asked. "Is he in on it too?"

Malik shook his head. "I'm not sure. Look, we have to get out of here. Katya, after you texted me that you were coming up here, I kinda told SL."

Luke stared at Katya, who said, "Hey, I didn't know." She then turned to Malik. "You told SL that we were coming up here?"

"I... I didn't know what to do. SL has been really good to us and she promised me a really good job with the bigger hotel and that maybe she would help me go somewhere else, maybe even help us to see Mom."

Katya stared disapprovingly at her brother.

"But as soon as I told her, I regretted it," Malik added. "I never wanted you to get involved, Katya. SL said it wouldn't be all that unusual if there was another accident at the fjord. I don't want anyone else to get hurt."

Ezzy's mind was reeling. She'd been right all along. Malik was in on it. But SL was definitely the mastermind, the real bad guy. Make that bad woman. Before she could even say I told you so, a thumping sound reverberated across the fjord. Ezzy, along with the others, turned upstream toward the glacier. A helicopter was flying their way, fast. It wasn't the red rescue helicopter. This one was sleek, black, and ominous looking.

"Uh oh," Malik moaned. "We have to get out of sight. Those are SL's goons."

"How about inside the shack?" Luke suggested.

"That's the first place they'll look," Malik replied. "Follow me, I have an idea."

Ezzy and Luke both turned to their father questioningly. He nodded. "Let's get under cover and then we can decide what to do next."

Ezzy wasn't ready to forgive Malik and still didn't trust him, but she figured they didn't have much choice right then. She followed the boy as he led them around to the back of the shack. The thumping sound of the helicopter grew louder. Malik scooted behind a locked wooden box like the one at the first shack and headed for a big gray rock atop the cliff at the fjord's edge. "Follow me and watch your step."

Malik crept carefully onto a natural rock stairway going down the cliff. "The researchers sometimes use this trail to the glacier and their camp." He went a little way down and then stopped under an overhang of rocks.

The others followed until they were all huddled under the rocky overhang. The helicopter was soon overhead. The wind from its rotating blades stirred up the dust around them. The group stood still and silent, flattened against the cliff. The helicopter seemed to be hovering above. Luke leaned out to take a peek, but Malik grabbed him and pulled him back under the overhang. Several long minutes later, the thumping of the helicopter began to fade.

"They can't land here," Malik told them. "But there's a spot not too far away where they can. They'll probably land there and then come to check out the shack. We'd better get out of here."

"Wait!" Ezzy said. "Why should we trust you?"

"My little sister's here," Malik snapped. "And besides, I already told you everything."

Dr. Skylar put a hand on Ezzy's shoulder. "It's okay, Ez. He knows the area and is probably our best bet to find a way back to town."

"They'll see us if we head back to town," Malik told them. "But we could go to the research camp. There should be a satellite phone there that works even this far out. And I know someone we can call to come get us."

Ezzy shook her head. "But I thought you said there were people working for SL at the camp."

"Yeah, those guys in the helicopter. If they're in the

helicopter, they are not at the camp. My friend's dad is with the local rescue squad, we can call him."

Dr. Skylar swatted something away from his face. "Are you sure there's no way back to town from here?"

"Not without being seen. Besides, that's where they'll expect you to head. They won't think you'd go to the camp."

Luke slapped something on his neck. "Ouch!"

The noise from the helicopter had disappeared. Ezzy figured it had landed. A new sound, however, had arisen—a loud, disconcerting buzzing around her head. Ezzy remembered the sign on the boardwalk warning of unusually large mosquitoes at dusk. She swatted the air. "I vote for going somewhere minus the giant blood-sucking bugs."

"That's another reason to head to the camp," Malik offered. "Fewer mosquitoes on the ice. This time of day they start coming out on land."

"So, we have a choice of humungous mosquitoes and bad guys, or the ice," said Luke. "I know I said no more hiking on the ice for me, but I vote for the camp even if it is on the glacier."

Dr. Skylar nodded. "Guess it's our best option."

Ezzy swatted an over-sized mosquito before it could land on her nose and glared at Malik. "Yeah, guess we don't have much choice *now.*"

Malik rolled his eyes at her and then went further down the cliff-side stairs to a ledge overlooking the fjord. Some fifty feet away stood a colossal vertical frozen cliff—the glacier's massive floating ice shelf. It towered over them. The Skylars stopped and stared only briefly as the buzzing of mosquitoes grew. Malik and Katya kept moving upstream along the narrow rock ledge.

"C'mon!" Malik yelled back. "They might see us from the shack."

The group skirted carefully but as quickly as possible around a boulder and then climbed as the trail ascended. The massive ice shelf to their right soon gave way to a field of fractured ice, lined with brown speckles of dirt and pebbles. Something darted across the trail ahead.

"What was that?" Luke called out while swatting the air to keep the mosquitoes away.

"Fox," Katya replied.

Something even smaller nearly ran over Ezzy's foot. She yelped and ran ahead.

Luke laughed. "I think that was a mouse, sis."

"More like a rat," she said, staring purposely at Malik.

"The research camp isn't too much farther," Malik told them.

About fifteen minutes and numerous mosquito bites later, Malik stopped. "From here we hike out over the glacier."

Dr. Skylar scanned the area around them. "Son,

this doesn't look like a very good place to hide if they come back in that helicopter."

Ezzy stared suspiciously at Malik.

"I know," the boy replied. "But it's a pretty short hike from here. Besides, they'll be looking the other way, thinking you went to town."

"I do remember seeing a satellite dish and communications gear when I was at the camp the other day during the rescue."

Malik stepped across a foot-wide crevasse and onto an area of brown pebbly ice. "Keep your eyes open and step where I step," he told them.

Katya followed her brother. Luke went next with Ezzy behind him and Dr. Skylar at the rear. They navigated around the glacier's giant crevasses and big holes. Ezzy tried to avoid looking down into their dark and scary depths. She also wondered how Malik knew which way to go until she realized they were on a path marked by small wooden stakes hammered into the ice.

They walked in silence. The buzz of mosquitoes had disappeared, and everyone's attention was focused on treading safely across the packed snow and ice. Clouds had drifted in overhead as the sun began to sink toward the horizon. It was still light out but getting dimmer, and the air temperature was dropping. Ezzy was glad she had on her hiking shoes and had brought a hat, gloves, and her especially long red scarf, which was now wrapped several times around her neck. She kept a caring eye on Luke and followed his every step.

Malik jogged ahead. "There's the camp, c'mon."

Ezzy looked up to see a scattering of heavy plastic crates, a few tents, and a weather station sitting atop the glacier. Two things surprised her. No people and a stack of yellow kayaks.

The group gathered in the center of the camp.

"Where are the scientists?" Luke asked.

"Uh, maybe they went into town for supplies, or something else happened," Malik replied. "Or to the hospital to visit that injured scientist. They usually come out for a couple of weeks at a time, but they do make periodic trips into town for stuff."

Dr. Skylar glanced around. "Where's the sat phone?"

"Well..." mumbled Malik. "Usually it's set up about where we're standing."

Ezzy eyed Malik, again wondering if they should trust him. Maybe he led them out there so the guys in the helicopter could come back and get them more easily.

"Maybe it's in one of the boxes," Katya suggested.

"Okay everyone, let's look for it," Dr. Skylar urged as he went to the nearest crate and opened it. "Not here. Mostly canned food in this one."

"Well at least we won't starve," Luke joked.

"Ha ha," said Ezzy as she went to the crate beside the kayaks and lifted the lid. Inside were paddles and some suits that resembled onesies made of black rubber. "Not here either."

After searching through the rest of the crates and the tents with no luck, the group again gathered on the packed snow at the center of the deserted research camp.

Malik shrugged. "I guess they might have taken the sat phone with them."

"Now, what?" asked Luke. "Should we hike back?"

Just then, the distant thumping of a helicopter echoed across the fjord.

"Maybe it's... the rescue helicopter," Luke suggested.

Malik shook his head. "Don't count on it."

Katya's chin quivered and her eyes began to well up. Malik reached tenderly for his sister and pulled her into a tight hug. "Don't worry, we'll figure something out. I won't let them hurt you."

"Yeah, you got us into this mess," Ezzy groaned.

"I know. I know," Malik responded. "You don't need to rub it in."

"Yeah," said Ezzy. "I kinda do."

"Okay, enough," said Dr. Skylar. He turned to Malik. "Are you absolutely sure these men mean us harm?"

"Yes."

"Then we need to find a way to get help or back to town asap, preferably without being seen." He turned again to Malik. "Any ideas?"

The thumping of the helicopter grew distinctly louder. Realizing the obvious—they were very visible standing out on the surface of the glacier—Ezzy, along with the others, scanned the area looking for an escape route or someplace to hide.

"Well, one idea," said Malik. "But it's kinda crazy."

"How crazy?" Ezzy asked. "Like a little nutso or sure to die whackadoodle bonkersville?"

"Not sure to die, but maybe."

In the distance, a black spec appeared in the sky.

"Well?" Dr. Skylar asked Malik.

Sprinting to the crate nearest the kayaks, the boy quickly lifted the lid and pulled out two halves of a take-apart paddle. "I've been helping shuttle the scientists and supplies back and forth from town. They showed me a map. They've discovered a network of rivers in tunnels inside the glacier and think they empty into the water in the fjord."

"Yeah," Luke said. "We heard about that."

"The other day they dumped some green dye and a float with a camera into one of the moulins. They tracked them inside the glacier and found the exit. They're planning to use the kayaks to go down a moulin and paddle on the rivers through the ice tunnels and out into the fjord."

"That is definitely crazy," Ezzy moaned.

Luke twirled his finger near his head. "Bonkers."

"No, I've seen the map and heard them talking about it," Malik told them. "They're convinced it will work. I think so too."

"And?" Dr. Skylar questioned.

"We could do it." Holding up the paddle and pointing into the crate. "Those are dry suits, so even if we get wet or fall in, we won't die... for at least a little while."

Ezzy rolled her eyes. "Oh, that makes me feel so much better."

The noise of the helicopter increased as it flew toward them.

Dr. Skylar shook his head. "That sounds extremely dangerous. I can't allow my kids to do that or you."

"My guess is these guys are gonna shove us into a crevasse anyway, and they have guns," Malik announced. "Around here, people disappear out on glaciers. It's not an uncommon thing. I vote for kayaking."

The black helicopter neared and a side door opened. A man inside slung a rifle around from across his back. As the aircraft swooped lower, the man aimed the gun at the group.

"Take cover! Get down!" shouted Dr. Skylar as he grabbed Luke and flung him to the ground behind the nearest crate.

Ezzy ran and dove behind the stack of kayaks.

Malik swept up Katya and hid behind another equipment box.

The helicopter swooped low over the group. Over the noise of the helicopter, Ezzy couldn't hear much, but suddenly she saw something ping into the ice in front of the kayaks. *The guy was shooting at them.* She gasped and ducked lower. The helicopter then began to hover and a voice from a loudspeaker echoed across the ice, "Do not move. Stay right where you are. We are going to land at the side of the glacier and then hike back. Stay here. Those shots were just to get your attention. We just want to talk to you."

The helicopter rose and headed across the glacier toward the coast.

Malik was the first to pop up from his hiding spot. "Don't believe them. If they don't shoot us, they'll push us into a crevasse or maybe both. Let's take the kayaks. We don't have much time."

Ezzy joined her father and Luke who had also come out of hiding.

"I think we should do it," Luke told his father.

Ezzy couldn't see the helicopter or men now, but she knew they were still out there. She figured they had fifteen, maybe twenty minutes at the most. She couldn't believe what she was about to say. "Me too. Let's go in the kayaks."

Standing close to Malik, Katya nodded.

"If anything happens to any of you, I will never forgive myself," Dr. Skylar groaned. "But if those men truly mean us harm, I don't see much choice."

Malik nodded. "Believe me, they do."

"How do we know which moulin to go into?" Dr. Skylar asked Malik.

"They marked it with dye." He pointed to a splotch of bright lime green next to a moulin about twenty-five feet away. A narrow stream of turquoise meltwater coming from higher up on the glacier flowed into the large hole.

From the crate, Malik began whipping out paddles and dry suits. "Hurry, put these on. They're big, but we can keep our jackets and shoes on underneath. Step into them and pull the neck over your head, like this. It zippers across the front." He showed them how the zipper closed across the top of his chest.

Hurrying, Malik helped Katya into a dry suit, while Dr. Skylar assisted Ezzy and Luke. Over their jackets and with their shoes on, the suits fit okay. Except for the length of the arms and legs. With them pushed up, the team resembled a collection of weird wrinkly black marshmallow people. It was a tight fit for Dr. Skylar, but he managed to squeeze into one of the dry suits as well. He put his backpack on over it.

As soon as everyone was geared up, Malik grabbed a paddle and the handle at the tip of a double kayak. He ran toward the patch of bright green on the ice, pulling the kayak behind him. Katya grabbed a paddle and raced after him. There were several more double kayaks and a few singles. Dr. Skylar grabbed the handles of a single and a double kayak and jogged after Malik. "Grab the paddles," he yelled to Ezzy and Luke.

Ezzy had suddenly become aware of how quiet it was. The helicopter had definitely landed. She looked toward the coast. In the distance, three, presumably armed men were running toward them.

At the dye patch, Malik positioned the double kayak's bow at the edge of a ramp carved into the moulin. It was no longer a vertical drop, but a gradual slope of ice going into the hole. "Get in," he urged Katya. Turning to the others he added, "Hurry. Follow us as close as you can and watch your heads. Oh, and I assume you can all swim if needed."

Katya hopped into the front seat of the kayak and Malik got in behind her. Ezzy and Luke helped their father line up the other two kayaks behind them. Ezzy really wanted to go with her father in the double kayak, but then Luke would be by himself. "I'll go in the single, Dad," she offered nervously.

"No. You two go in the double and I'll follow in the single. That way if something happens, I'll be right there."

Ezzy knew her father meant if she or Luke fell out or they capsized, but she didn't want to say that out loud. Her heart pounded and her trembling legs felt like rubbery noodles. She nodded and simply muttered, "Okay."

Dr. Skylar helped Luke into the front seat of the other double kayak, while Ezzy jumped in the back.

He handed each a paddle. "Remember when we went kayaking on the Potomac River at home. It'll be just like that."

Yeah, just like that, Ezzy thought. *Only a bajillion degrees colder and scarier.*

The men from the helicopter were nearly upon them. From across their backs, they pulled their rifles forward. "Stop!" one of them yelled. "Stop right there."

Dr. Skylar shoved Malik and Katya's kayak forward. It hit the inclined ice and slid downward.

"Here we go!" shouted Malik.

"I love you both so much," Dr. Skylar said to his kids. "Be careful and I'll be right behind you." He then shoved the second kayak with Ezzy and Luke in it onto and down the ice ramp. Without waiting to watch as they disappeared into the moulin, he pushed his kayak right to the edge of the ramp. Holding his paddle, Dr. Skylar jumped in. His weight tipped the kayak downward and it descended into the moulin and under the ice.

* * *

A Wild Ride

E zzy figured their chances of dying were, on a scale from one to ten—a twenty. But she had no time to worry about it. The kayak she and Luke were in had slid swiftly down the water-slickened ice ramp into the moulin. Inside, the light was an eerie blue. Shadows flickered on the surrounding walls. As Ezzy and Luke tightened their grip on their paddles, the slope steepened, and their kayak picked up speed.

Inside the glacier, meltwater flowing into and down the moulins converged and had created a fast-flowing-turbulent river. The kayaks now raced along with it inside the ice tunnel.

"Woohoo!" shouted Luke.

Ezzy screamed too, but not with joy or abandon,

more like sheer terror. What had she been thinking? Only lunatics would attempt what they were doing. She kept her eyes on Malik and Katya's kayak racing ahead of them and prayed her father was close behind.

Malik shouted back, "Duck and lean right!"

Ezzy and Luke bent forward just in time. The ceiling lowered and the ice tunnel curved left. As their kayak raced around the tight turn, Ezzy and Luke leaned to the right. If they hadn't, Ezzy was sure they would have flipped over. The kayak righted and raced into a straightaway. They flew with the roiling rushing water, rocking from side to side. Suddenly, the kayak in front disappeared. Katya screamed. *That can't be good*, thought Ezzy. Their kayak struck a hump in the underlying ice and bounced. Next thing Ezzy knew they were flying through the air.

"When you land, paddle hard!" yelled Malik.

Their kayak hit the water and Luke and Ezzy paddled as if their life depended on it, which it probably did. They glided forward just as their father's kayak shot out of the ice tunnel and landed right behind them. With the rush of adrenaline, Ezzy felt shaky, yet hyper-alert.

Ezzy caught her breath and tried to make sense of her surroundings. As her eyes adjusted to the darkness, she made out faint hints of light illuminating where they'd landed. They were floating on a lake inside a giant cavern in the ice. Ezzy couldn't tell how deep or big the lake was. She and Luke paddled up to Malik and Katya, and soon their father joined them.

"Whoa!" said Luke. "That was awesome."

This time it was Ezzy who felt a little woozy. "Aren't you the same kid that gets carsick?"

"It's not the same, Ez. That was like an awesome water slide at an amusement park."

"Well," noted their father. "This is no amusement park and I think we are lucky to be alive."

"Yeah," offered Malik. "Thanks to me."

"Oh brother," groaned Ezzy. "We're in the dark, in kayaks on a lake under tons of ice, almost died, and there are bad guys chasing us." She looked back toward the round opening in the ice behind them. "You want to take credit for that?"

"Speaking of which," her father added. "Let's try to find a way out of here."

"If I remember the map right," Malik told them. "It showed a couple of under-the-ice rivers going out the other side of this cavern." He pointed into the darkness. "That way."

The lake's dark surface was calm and the air cold. Ezzy squinted, trying to make out the far wall of the cavern. Then, she glanced up. The ceiling was faintly lit and at least fifty feet above their heads. They began paddling toward the other side of the lake and cavern. In the wake behind Malik and Katya's kayak, Ezzy was surprised to see shimmering sparkles of light.

"Do you think anything lives down here?" Luke questioned.

"Maybe," his father answered.

Ezzy glanced around nervously. "Like what?"

Before anyone could guess, they saw a more distinct, V-shaped glow rippling in the water. The shape reminded Ezzy of a flock of birds flying south for the winter. Then she realized something must be below the glittering water and it was headed straight for them.

"Uh oh," she muttered as she began stroking backward, her old fear of wild animals filling her stomach with knots like a burger gone bad. Ezzy imagined that below the surface swam an enormous shark or some sort of sea monster. *An Arctic kraken?*

Malik and Katya stopped paddling. Ezzy and Luke's kayak collided with their father's. They all watched as whatever was under the water got closer. Ezzy shut her eyes, scared to see what was approaching. Then Luke started giggling. She raised one eyelid. A little whiskered face floated beside their kayak staring up at Luke. Ezzy opened both eyes. It was a spotted gray seal, like the one they'd seen the other day. It bobbed up and down, peering at them, or more specifically at her little brother.

Ezzy sighed in relief. "It's a seal."

"It must have swum up here from the fjord," Malik noted. "That means there's definitely a way out."

The seal jumped onto the bow of Luke and Ezzy's kayak. Once the kayak stopped rocking, the seal lay down, rubbed its whiskered snout on the kayak, and faced forward.

"Looks like you have a friend," Dr. Skylar said to Luke.

"As usual," Ezzy added.

They began paddling again toward the other side of the cavern. A few minutes later, a loud splashing sound came from behind. Ezzy stopped paddling and looked back, but in the darkness behind them she couldn't see anything. Although she hoped she was wrong, Ezzy figured it was one of the men from the helicopter. He'd probably taken another of the kayaks and followed them. Darn, she thought, they should have dumped the other kayaks or at least the remaining paddles in a moulin or crevasse. Then again, it was easy to think of that now, but not so easy back then when they'd been running for their lives.

"Let's keep going," Dr. Skylar urged.

The seal slid off the kayak and swam ahead effortlessly, leaving behind a trail of sparkling light.

"Follow the seal," Luke urged.

Ezzy shrugged. The follow-the-animal thing had worked for them in the past.

Malik and Katya paddled beside Ezzy and Luke trailing the seal. Dr. Skylar remained at the back. No one spoke as they concentrated on following the shimmering wake of their flippered blubbery guide. It glided silently just below the surface, periodically stopping to bob up and look back at the group.

Soon Ezzy heard a strange noise, almost like running water. She looked around but couldn't tell where the sound was coming from.

Ahead of them, the seal's sparkling wake veered to the left. With strong, sure strokes of his paddle, Malik turned their kayak to follow. Ezzy and Luke paddled on their right to turn left as well. But their kayak continued going straight. Then it began to drift to the right.

"Left," urged their father. "Paddle left."

"We're trying," Ezzy said, paddling hard on her right to force the kayak left. But something seemed to be pulling them to the right. The noise she'd heard grew louder. It reminded Ezzy of something, but she wasn't sure what. She glanced ahead. Across the water lay a distinct and shimmering line.

Luke stared ahead. "What's that?"

"I think it's a... a..."

"Waterfall," Malik finished for her.

Ahead, water cascaded over a steep drop, creating a glowing line at the surface and a strong current. Too strong. It was pulling Ezzy and Luke's kayak toward it. As they were pulled closer, the sound of the waterfall intensified.

Malik twisted around in his kayak. "Look for a line or rope. Something we can use to pull you."

Still paddling as hard as they could, Ezzy and Luke looked about the kayak. Luke shook his head. "Nothing here. Hurry, it's taking us."

Ezzy felt a bump and their kayak was knocked sideways away from the waterfall or as she suddenly thought of it—the falls of certain death. Using his kayak and paddling in strong strokes, her father was pushing them to the left. They weren't going toward the waterfall anymore, but they weren't getting further away either. Then Ezzy had an idea. "Luke, keep paddling."

"What do you think I'm doing!"

As quickly as she could Ezzy tucked her paddle under one arm and unwrapped the long red scarf from around her neck. She balled up one end and threw it to Katya, who had drifted closer in the other kayak.

"Got it!" said Katya, catching the tip of the scarf and passing it to Malik.

"You're kidding, right?" Malik shouted to Ezzy.

"No," Ezzy replied as she passed her end of the scarf to Luke and began paddling again. "Tie it on. It'll work. I know it."

As Dr. Skylar continued to paddle hard, keeping Ezzy and Luke's kayak from drifting to the left, Luke leaned forward and tied the scarf to the handle on the front of their kayak. Meanwhile, while shaking his head in doubt, Malik tied the other end of the scarf to the back of their kayak. He and Katya then began stroking. The scarf stretched but held. Soon, all three kayaks began to slowly move away from the waterfall.

"See!" Ezzy said smugly to Malik.

"Yeah, guess you were right. This time."

"Geez," muttered Ezzy, but inside she was gloating. *Eat that*, she said silently to Malik and everyone else that had ever teased her about wearing her mother's scarves. Not only had one helped to save Katya's puppy, this one just saved her and Luke from the falls of certain death.

In the distance behind them, a man shouted, "You can't escape. We know where this comes out!"

While continuing to paddle, Luke and Ezzy turned nervously to their father.

"If that was true," he told them, "why would he be following us?"

Luke nodded, but Ezzy wasn't so sure.

"Hey, where'd the seal go?" Katya said from up front.

The sparkling trail they'd been following had disappeared. In the distance, however, it looked a little brighter. Ezzy thought it might be the other side of the cavern. She prayed there was an exit. Ezzy couldn't decide which would be worse, getting stuck under hundreds of tons of ice or running into SL's armed and dangerous goon. Even worse would be both. Searching for any sign of the seal or an exit, she and the others paddled ahead.

Minutes later, Ezzy got the distinct feeling they had picked up speed. "Stop paddling for a second," she said to Luke.

He held up his paddle. Their kayak continued to glide forward.

"Uh, we're being pulled again," Luke observed. "Is there another waterfall ahead?"

A faint glow and the sloping wall of the cavern came into view, but there was no shimmering line like before.

Up ahead, Katya and Malik's kayak tilted downward. Katya screamed, and again they disappeared from sight.

"Hang on!" Ezzy shouted as their kayak angled downward.

Connected by the scarf, the two kayaks plummeted into another ice tunnel. They raced downstream atop another swiftly flowing inside-the-ice river. It was darker in this tunnel, which twisted and turned like a snake winding its way through the grass. Tied to the one ahead, Ezzy and Luke's kayak weaved and tilted wildly. On one particularly sharp bend, they nearly tipped over. To prevent being tossed out, Ezzy and Luke grabbed onto both sides of the kayak. In the process, they dropped their paddles, which were immediately swept away by the surrounding rush and swirl of white water.

Atop the river, the kayaks raced through rapids and careened around turns. Freezing water splashed and poured into the narrow boats. Without the dry suits, the group would have been hypothermic and already on death's doorstep.

Peering through the spray of freezing water, Ezzy suddenly realized she could better see Malik and Katya ahead. It was getting brighter inside the ice tunnel. Then, as if shooting off a water slide, one after another the kayaks flew out of the ice tunnel and into the dim evening light.

After she stopped shaking and gave thanks for not falling out, not drowning, not losing a limb, and still being alive, Ezzy glanced around. They had landed in the fjord in calm water, in front of the glacier's massive ice shelf. To their left was a cliff-lined coast. It was the southern, more remote side of the fjord.

Malik pumped his fist. "Yes!" Turning to Ezzy, he added, "See, I told you it would work."

Ezzy rolled her eyes and stared back at the colossal ice shelf. The tunnel's exit was a large dark hole in the vertical face of the frozen cliff.

Luke stared back at the shelf and grinned. "We just shot out of the glacier's butt hole!"

The tension built up during the intense experience in the ice tunnels broke, and everyone laughed.

"Then that really was a poop chute," Ezzy added. "And we were the poop."

They all laughed some more. It was a classic case of the giggles.

"Glad someone remembered to flush," Dr. Skylar said.

They laughed even harder.

Dr. Skylar took a deep breath to compose himself and then turned to the group. "C'mon, let's put some distance between us and this ice."

Ezzy added, "Yeah and that guy that may be coming out behind us."

"Maybe he'll get stuck or go the wrong way," Luke suggested hopefully.

"Let's not be here to find out," his father responded. "Start paddling."

* * *

Climb Aboard

I n the calm water in front of the ice shelf and next to the coast, Malik and Katya began to paddle using their kayak to pull Ezzy and Luke in theirs. Dr. Skylar took up the rear.

"Hey, hold up," Luke told them, pointing off to their left.

"Another seal?" Malik asked, rolling his eyes.

"Hey, that seal saved us," Luke said. "No. It's our paddles."

Bobbing in the water nearby were two paddles.

"Pull us over," Ezzy urged.

"I'll get them," Dr. Skylar offered. After quickly grabbing the paddles, he brought them to Ezzy and Luke. "Here you go."

Malik had already untied the scarf from their kayak and tossed the end to Luke. Ezzy began stroking as Luke put his paddle across the kayak before untying the other end of the scarf. He passed it back to Ezzy and resumed paddling.

The group headed downstream along the coast. Before long, they came to the massive jam of icebergs in the middle of the fjord.

"There's no way around," Malik said. "We'll have to go through."

"Look for areas of open water," Dr. Skylar told them.

Malik and Katya took the lead, weaving their way around and among the icebergs. In some places the kayaks barely fit between the massive blocks of ice. In other spots, they had to push aside small frozen chunks. All the while, the group watched warily for falling ice or icebergs that could tip over onto them. Ezzy knew it was a perilous journey, but compared to the rapids in the ice tunnel, it felt pretty tame. Then she realized how ridiculous that was. Perspective, Ezzy thought. It's all about perspective and hers was clearly totally messed up. She prayed there wouldn't be a big collapse upstream or they'd be goners for sure.

A loud crack echoed across the fjord followed by a distinct splash. They all stopped and scanned the area but didn't see where the ice had split or fallen.

"Let's keep going," Dr. Skylar urged.

Malik paddled harder, leading them around a car-sized iceberg bobbing gently in the water. Ezzy eyed it guardedly as she and Luke passed by. She looked up and saw where Malik and Katya were headed. "Ah... is there another way around?"

Malik turned back. "Nope."

"But that could collapse any minute. We've seen it happen."

"Then you better make it through fast," Malik told her, before he and Katya headed under an iceberg shaped like an arched bridge. They stroked strongly, moving the kayak swiftly under the archway. Seconds later, Katya yelled back, "It's fine. Go for it!"

Ezzy looked back to her father, who nodded encouragingly.

"After this, I never want to see another piece of ice again," Ezzy groaned. "Ready, Luke?"

"I was born ready."

Dr. Skylar chuckled as Ezzy rolled her eyes before saying, "Oh, just go."

They paddled hard. The kayak slid forward. Ezzy stared straight ahead not wanting to look up at the ice and see any cracks or pieces about to fall. Under the arch it was cooler and dark. Ezzy could swear she heard cracking. Seconds later they popped out the other side.

"Look!" Luke shouted, pointing behind Malik and Katya who had turned their kayak around to watch them. "It's a boat."

Dr. Skylar made it through the iceberg arch and joined them. Everyone stared at the boat in the distance.

"It's the *Ice Maiden 2*," Katya said. "They must be on an evening trip."

"Head that way," Dr. Skylar told them.

The group began paddling toward the boat. Ezzy stroked toward the vessel but was wary. Could they trust Anders, the boat captain? Maybe he was in on the whole melt-the-glacier-thing. And where was the guy who'd been following them?

The *Ice Maiden 2* cruised alongside a peaked iceberg full of fractures. Luke stared that way. "What if they don't see us and leave?"

"No worries there," his father answered as he stopped paddling and pulled off his backpack. "I've got something that should do the trick."

The others watched as he rummaged through his pack. He pulled something out and paddled to Luke and Ezzy. "I believe you two know how to use one of these." He handed it to Ezzy.

Luke grinned. "You're the best, Dad."

Ezzy nodded, pulled the top off the flare, and held it high over her head. Sparks flew out and a stream of orange smoke rose skyward. "Someone has to see it."

A few minutes later they heard the blast of the *Ice Maiden 2's* horn. They headed for the ship as it began to slowly turn their way. Ezzy looked behind the group, again wondering what had happened to the guy who had followed them into the ice tunnel. There was still no sign of the man.

The kayakers exited the Kangia Icefjord as the *Ice Maiden 2* coasted to a stop nearby. Elise, the deckhand, lowered the rope ladder. Malik and Katya positioned their kayak next to the ship's hull directly beneath the ladder.

"You first," Malik told Katya as he held onto the ladder to keep the kayak steady.

She stood up and wavered a little. Katya then grabbed the ladder and climbed out of the kayak. Elise threw a long line to Malik. He tied it to the tip of his kayak and then waved Luke and Ezzy over to tie their kayak on as well. Afterward, he leapt out of the kayak onto the ladder. Luke and Ezzy paddled next to the boat. Ezzy held onto the ladder to keep their kayak steady like Malik had. "You're next," she told Luke.

Luke stood up and scurried up the ladder. Ezzy threw the line from their kayak to her father to tie his kayak on. Then it was Ezzy's turn to climb out. The bulky dry suit made it hard to maneuver, but Ezzy was more than ready to be out of the kayak. She made it up nearly as fast as her little brother. Dr. Skylar went last. Once they were all aboard, Elise, Anders, and the hotel guests helped each of them out of their dry suits. They were given warm blankets and steaming cups of chicken noodle soup. Then the questions started.

Malik and Katya hung back and stayed silent. Ezzy and Luke began to explain what had happened, but their father quickly held up his hand, indicating for them to stop. "We need to contact the local authorities," he told Anders.

"What happened?"

"We'd prefer not to say right here," Dr. Skylar answered, nodding toward his kids.

"First off, I'd better call Hendrik and Anguk to let them know you're all okay?"

"No!" shouted Ezzy. "I mean yes, call Katya and Malik's father to let him know they're okay, but not Hendrik."

"Not Hendrik?" Anders asked. "Why?"

"Actually," said Dr. Skylar. "Why don't you call Hendrik and have him and his wife, SL, meet us at the dock. Along with the police."

Katya hugged Malik and whispered, "Don't worry. I'll tell the police you helped save us."

Anders told Elise to tie the line towing the kayaks to a cleat on the stern. He then radioed ahead to the police and made the call to Hendrik.

Ezzy peered out over the stern toward the iceberg mash-up in the fjord. She wasn't sure, but in the distance it looked like a lone kayak had just popped out from under the iceberg archway.

* * *

20

Simply Unbelievable

E zzy stood at the stern rail as the *Ice Maiden 2* cruised into the Ilulissat village inlet. A small crowd had gathered at the dock. Blue lights flashed atop the roofs of several cars parked alongside. "Do you see Hendrik or SL?" she asked her father.

"Hard to tell from here."

"Maybe they'll make a run for it," Luke suggested.

"And go where?" Ezzy responded.

Luke shrugged.

"Dad," Ezzy said. "I just want to say, you should have believed us about the pipe and steam. I mean, I feel bad about the whole thing with Anguk, though he is a scary dude, but Luke and I were right all along about the other stuff."

Her father nodded. "I'm sorry, Ezzy. You're right. Those men in the helicopter were chasing us and Malik confirmed what you said was going on. I should have believed you and your brother. But as we've learned on this trip, we all make mistakes and must learn from them. And that includes me."

"It's okay, Dad," Luke announced. "I forgive you."

He said it so seriously that Ezzy laughed and her father chuckled before saying. "Thanks, bud. You both were amazingly brave kayaking under the ice. And Ezzy, that was really quick thinking, using the scarf as a tow line near that waterfall."

Ezzy smiled. She was both surprised and proud of how well she'd done hiking across the icebergs and in their wild inside-the-ice kayak trip. The idea to use the scarf had popped into her head out of nowhere. When she thought too much about things, she got scared and insecure. But if it all happened quickly and she didn't have any time to think or worry about it, she could do things she never imagined. Ezzy remembered her mom telling her she needed to get out of her own head. She had to trust and believe in herself more. Then she thought—maybe the new, adventurous Ezzy wasn't just a one-time fluke in the Galápagos, it really was who she was.

Anders was soon maneuvering the ship alongside the dock. It was late evening, but still light out and the air was cool with a salty, seaweedy smell. Elise threw the bow line to a policeman on the dock. He wrapped it fast around a cleat. She jogged back and jumped off the boat with the stern line in hand before rapidly securing it to another cleat.

As soon as the boat was tied up, Anguk leapt aboard and ran to Katya. He hugged her tight and reached for Malik.

"Hold on!" commanded Anders, walking onto the stern deck. "No one else on or off, before I say so. I'm still the captain here. This is my ship."

"Make that my ship," proclaimed a voice with authority from shore.

"Uh yes, Hendrik, technically that's true," Anders replied. "But while folks are aboard, the captain is in charge."

An older, stocky man with swept back gray hair in a uniform stepped forward. "As chief of police, I'll say when and if anyone gets off this ship. Now, what exactly is going on and what is this about an attempted assault up on the glacier?"

Dr. Skylar came forward. "We're the ones who called it in. These other folks had nothing to do with it. Please let them go, and we'll speak with you privately."

The police chief nodded to Anders, who thanked his guests, wished them well and encouraged them to disembark. Another worker from the hotel had arrived to drive them back. Meanwhile, the chief and a female police officer, along with Hendrik and SL, boarded the ship. They followed the others still aboard into the ship's cabin. Elise brought hot drinks as the group seated themselves around a table.

"Now, who would like to start?" asked the police chief.

"It all started when we found the pipe," Luke jumped in.

"The *hot* pipe," Ezzy added, staring at SL.

Dr. Skylar raised his hand. "Hold on. Let me explain." He proceeded to tell the officers about his kids finding the pipe and that they believed someone was pumping hot water into the fjord to make the glacier melt faster. And that at first, even though he didn't really believe it, he humored them by going up to the science shack. He then recounted how Malik had shown up and how the men in the helicopter had threatened them with guns. And how they ended up using the kayaks to escape through the ice tunnels.

No one spoke during Dr. Skylar's recounting of what had happened, but there were several gasps and numerous looks of disbelief.

"Uh... that sounds pretty unbelievable," the female officer offered.

"You're telling me," Luke responded.

Dr. Skylar gave him a quick hug. "I know, but that's exactly what happened."

"Who were the men?" the chief questioned.

Ezzy and Luke turned pointedly to SL and Hendrik. "Ask them," Ezzy said.

"Us?" Hendrik replied. "Why us? How would we know?"

"They're your men," accused Ezzy. "You're the ones melting the glacier so more people will come to your hotel. So you can get money to make it bigger and build a fancy schmancy spa."

Luke turned to Malik. "He told us everything."

Now the group's focus was on Malik. "I... uh... yeah, kinda told them everything. But then I helped them. I'd seen the map of the tunnels. It was my suggestion to use the kayaks. I saved them. It wasn't my fault."

The woman officer chimed in. "Okay, so who's fault is it? Who were the men with the guns?"

Malik bowed his head and pointed to SL.

SL put a hand to her chest. "Me?"

Inside the boat's cabin, SL's perfume was once again overwhelming. Amidst a sneeze, Ezzy said, "Yes, ach... you."

"I don't know what you all are talking about. I had nothing to do with this fantastical story. Right, Hendrik? We know nothing about any of this?"

Hendrik appeared even more shocked than his wife. "Absolutely. This is absurd. Yes, we are expanding the hotel and building a spa. There have been a few financial hurdles. But we have investors. Right, honey?"

"Of course," SL answered.

Ezzy glared in anger. "That's because you assured them the glacier here is melting faster than anywhere else and will bring in crowds."

"We heard you," added Luke.

"Absurd," responded SL.

"Look, in the past few days," Hendrik told the group. "There have been a number of serious misunderstandings. Luckily no one has been injured, but honestly, this has got to stop."

Glancing at Malik, SL chimed in. "Yes, that's right. Our men have been helping the scientists, and they always have rifles for protection and seal hunting. I think this just is another enormous misunderstanding."

"Ask him," Ezzy said, staring at Malik.

"Son, do you know anything about this?" Anguk asked.

Malik hesitated. Silence filled the room.

"Son?" Anguk repeated.

"Tell them," Katya said to her brother.

"They're telling the truth. I'm sorry SL, but I had to tell them."

Malik then recounted how SL had ordered him and several of her men to construct the heat pump system when they built the shacks and to keep an eye on the researchers. He then confirmed everything the Skylars had said.

Hendrik's eyes grew wide as he stared at his wife. "Is this true?"

"No, of course not," SL pleaded. "It's just hearsay

from folks with vivid imaginations and a young boy they've confused with their wild tales. We built the shacks for science and the pumps bring water up for drinking. There's no evidence to confirm any of this. There's nothing."

"But there is," Ezzy said. "There's a second shack and pumping system. Someone covered up the evidence at the first shack. But there's a second one."

"Yeah," Luke added.

Malik nodded.

"Well, we certainly can't do anything without some sort of evidence or proof," said the chief. He unhooked a radio from his belt and made a call. "I know this sounds crazy, but could you get a team as quickly as possible up to a wood hut next to the glacier and see if there is a system to pump heated water into the fjord. I'll get you the exact coordinates. Yes, I already told you it sounds crazy, just do it."

*   *   *

Frozen Frustration

While awaiting word from the team sent to investigate the second science shack, the police had escorted the group from the ship back to the hotel. The Skylars now sat in the restaurant off to one side, while Anguk stood nearby with Katya and Malik. Hendrik and SL were huddled and whispering to one another at the front of the restaurant. The hotel owners were calm, but clearly angry. They remained steadfast in their denial and continued to express shock at the accusations made against them.

The chief's radio crackled. He grabbed it from his belt. "Go ahead, Matt." Walking away from the group, he held the radio to his ear listening. The others watched and waited. The man nodded, said something into the radio and then returned it to his belt. He strode back to the group. "That was my officers reporting back from the second shack."

"Did they find the pipe?" Luke blurted out.

The officer nodded. "Yes, they did find a pumping system."

Luke and Ezzy sat forward hopefully.

"But there was no heater connected to it. It was a simple pump to bring cold water up from the fjord, just as Mrs. Rise here said."

"What?" exclaimed Ezzy.

"I'm sorry, but they found nothing to indicate that hot water was being pumped back into the fjord."

Disappointment rocked Ezzy. Luke's mouth fell open.

Then Ezzy thought about the men in the helicopter. "I bet that while that one guy chased us in the kayaks, the others went back and got rid of the evidence."

Luke nodded. "Yeah."

The chief turned to SL and Hendrik. "I'm so very sorry to have wasted your time and for the accusations. We've always had a good relationship. I hope this unfortunate incident won't change that."

"No worries," SL said sweetly. "It's just a big misunderstanding. We've had a lot of those lately." She raised an eyebrow at the Skylars.

"But Dad," Luke whispered. "We weren't making it up."

"I know, son. Officer, those men in the helicopter threatened us. They actually shot at us."

"I'm very sorry it seemed that way," the chief told them. "But with no solid evidence, your story just doesn't hold up."

The two officers shook hands with Hendrik and SL and headed to the hotel exit.

"But..." Ezzy moaned.

SL stood and slowly smoothed her pink cashmere sweater. She sighed and strode over to the Skylars. Ezzy's nose tingled.

"No hard feelings," the woman said though she pointedly glanced toward Malik. "Let's just chalk this up to another very unfortunate mix-up."

"Yes," added Hendrik, reading to leave. "Strange things happen this far north, and we'll just add this to the list. We hope you'll enjoy the rest of your stay, but please, no more wild adventures out on the ice or fairy tales."

Ezzy couldn't believe it. They were going to get away with it. And they were making her whole family, even her father, look awful and like idiots. It was completely unfair. "It wasn't a big misunderstanding. Just because we're kids doesn't mean we make things up or have a *vivid* imagination," Ezzy told them. "Someday the truth will come out."

Just then, Dr. Maggie Dixon entered the dining room, moving slowly on crutches. She was followed by her colleague Dr. Johnson and the two police officers who had just left.

"That day is right now," Maggie Dixon announced.

"Look who we ran into on our way out," said the chief of police. "They happen to mention some very strange results in their data. Mr. and Mrs. Rise, why don't you have a seat."

Hendrik and SL hesitated but then sat down.

"What sort of results?" Dr. Skylar asked.

"I'll let the scientists explain," the chief answered.

"You'd better do it," Maggie Dixon said, looking squarely at SL. "I'm a little out of breath and need to sit down *due to my accident.*"

Dr. Johnson stood in front of the others. "For several years now, we've been monitoring and investigating the retreat and melting of the glacier. We've been collecting data at the surface but also from below. As it turns out, we discovered that warm ocean water has been welling up into the fjord during the summer and melting the underside of the ice shelf. You see, the ice pressure is high due to all that weight, so it decreases the temperature of melting. At about..."

"We're not here for a science lesson," the chief interjected. "Get to it, man."

"As I was saying, the ice shelf is being melted by upwelling warm ocean water in the summer. But we found something very strange. When we combined the data from our strings of instruments placed on the seabed in the fjord with the temperature sensors on an AUV we recently deployed..."

"That's an autonomous underwater vehicle," Maggie added.

"Right," Dr. Johnson continued. "In addition to the upwelling, we discovered two distinct point sources of underwater heat. And they were not where we expected. It turns out they coincided very distinctly with two locations."

"Where?" asked Ezzy hopefully.

"Directly behind the two science shacks at the side of the fjord."

"Yes!" said Luke pumping his fist into the air.

"What?" roared Hendrik. "That can't be."

"I'm afraid it is," said Maggie. "Our data suggests that hot water has been intermittently entering the fjord at those two locations and we can find no natural explanation. And from what the chief just told us, we agree with what young Ezzy and Luke here have been saying. Someone has been periodically pumping hot water into the fjord. And it's causing the ice shelf to melt and collapse even faster than it already was. And this, of course, allows the glacier to travel faster and melt more."

"Mr. and Mrs. Rise, do you have anything to say?" the chief asked.

"I can assure you," replied Hendrik. "We had no knowledge of this or anything to do with it."

"Maybe it's geothermal heat," SL suggested.

The scientists simply shook their heads.

The chief and the woman officer then approached SL and Hendrik. "I think the two of you better come with us to the station."

"This is ridiculous," Hendrik announced. "We would never do what you are suggesting." He turned to his wife. "Right, honey?"

She stood stony-faced and silent.

The police officers left with Mr. and Mrs. Rise, Malik and Anguk, along with the scientists, and headed to the police station. Before going, the chief of police thanked the Skylars for all of their efforts and apologized for what they'd been through. Katya, in tears, had clung to her father. After he assured her everything would be okay and he would see her soon, the Skylars had stepped forward. Luke took Katya's hand, while Dr. Skylar offered to look after her while Anguk was getting things straightened out with Malik.

As the group headed back to the Skylars' hotel room, Katya asked, "Do you think Malik will get in trouble?"

Dr. Skylar put a comforting hand on the girl. "He helped us and told the truth. That should count for something and make a difference in whatever happens."

"What about Hendrik and SL?" Ezzy asked. "What do you think will happen to them?"

"I'm not sure," her father answered. "I don't know how things work around here."

"Do you think Hendrik was in on it the whole time?" Luke asked. "He seemed really nice."

Dr. Skylar shook his head. "Son, I just don't know."

*   *   *

An Icy Ending

The next morning Ezzy woke up to find Luke's bed empty and sunlight streaming in from around the edges of the curtains. She hopped up and peeked outside. It was a bright sunny day. She opened the bedroom door. Luke, Katya, and her father were eating breakfast in the sitting room. Katya had spent the night, sleeping on the couch.

Dr. Skylar looked up and smiled. "There she is, sleepyhead."

"What time is it?" Ezzy asked.

"Just past eleven. Thought we'd let you sleep."

"Thanks." Ezzy grabbed a blueberry muffin from a plate on the center coffee table. "What's going on?" She turned to Katya. "Any word from your dad?"

"He called. They got home really late and didn't want to wake us."

"Is Malik in jail with SL and Hendrik?"

Katya shook her head. "No, because he helped us, he got... something called impunity."

"That's immunity," Dr. Skylar corrected, chuckling. "Because he told the truth and helped us, they're not charging him with anything. But he did get community service hours, which means he'll be shoveling more puppy poop and doing good for some time."

"What about Hendrik and SL?" asked Ezzy.

"As it turns out," her father answered. "Hendrik was innocent. He had nothing to do with the whole crazy melt-the-glacier scheme, Maggie's accident or our misadventures. It was all SL. She devised elaborate ways to keep it from her husband."

"What's going to happen to her?"

"Not sure," Dr. Skylar answered. "But at least *we* won't have to worry about SL Rise anymore."

Luke's eyes widened and he giggled.

"What?" Ezzy asked.

"Yes, what's so funny?" his father added.

"SL Rise," Luke said. "I heard about SL rise in science class." He paused. "*Sea level rise.*"

"OMG, you're right," Ezzy said, laughing.

Dr. Skylar chuckled. "You know what they say, fact is stranger than weird coincidence."

"*Dad...* it's fact is stranger than fiction," Luke corrected.

"That too. So, we have one day left here. What do you want to do?"

"No kayaking," Ezzy announced.

"No helicopters," Luke added and then turned to Katya. "Can we go see the puppies?"

"Sure," she said. "Besides, I need to feed them."

They finished breakfast and headed out to the puppy pen behind the hotel. Katya unlocked the gate and they went inside. From the doghouse three balls of fur rushed out, yipping happily. This time Luke was prepared. He dropped to the ground so they wouldn't bowl him over. The puppies swarmed him. Loud giggling ensued, making the rest of the group laugh.

"I heard you were out here," said Hendrik, walking toward them. His clothes were rumpled, and his face looked haggard as if he hadn't slept all night. "I wanted to apologize in person. I had absolutely no idea what my wife was up to. I cannot believe what she did. It's truly shocking and I feel like an idiot for not being aware of what was going on. I cannot say how sorry I am for all that she put you through. Around here, we definitely don't want climate change to occur any faster than it is. It's bad enough already with all the permafrost thawing and ice getting thinner in the winter."

Dr. Skylar reached out to shake the man's hand. "Thank you. We appreciate that. And we're sorry for what you must be going through."

Hendrik shook his head. "I think I'm still in shock. I mean I knew she could be aggressive business-wise but had no idea of the lengths she would go to."

"What's going to happen to her?" Luke asked.

"Well, son, she made a terrible, awful mistake," Hendrik replied.

"Mistake?" Ezzy exclaimed. "She almost got us killed and Dr. Dixon. It wasn't a mistake. That's like me getting a math problem wrong."

Hendrik nodded. "Yes, yes. I didn't mean to make light of it. She did some terrible things. Part of me would like to think she was just overwhelmed by the thought of losing the hotel and everyone losing their jobs and got carried away."

"Carried away?" Ezzy groaned. "No! She literally tried to murder people."

"Ezzy, now, let's stay calm," her father told her.

"SL is going to pay for what she did," Hendrik told them. "Including some jail time, and then she'll probably be exiled from the country."

"What about the hotel?" Katya asked. "Is my dad going to lose his job?"

Hendrik stepped over and wrapped the girl in his arms. "Of course not, Katya. Anguk will always have a job as long as I am in charge." Winking at Ezzy, he added, "Though he may need to work on his people skills."

Ezzy nodded before asking, "Are you going to have to close?"

"No. We got the investors. In fact, I spoke to them this morning because there's been a change in plans."

"How so?" Dr. Skylar questioned.

"Instead of the spa across the road, we're going to build a research and education center. It will focus on the Kangia Icefjord and climate change. And be for the local community as well as visitors." Hendrik stepped back and crouched down in front of Katya. "Your dad and Malik are going to help. Would you like to be involved too?"

"Yes, please."

"That's a fantastic idea," Dr. Skylar noted. "And we'd like to help also."

"What do you mean?" Hendrik asked. "You've all been through enough, and you helped uncover what was really going on. What my soon-to-be ex-wife was up to."

"My wife's family left her an inheritance. We've been using it to travel to all of the places in the world she considered extraordinary and wanted to visit. It was what she called her wonder list. Ilulissat and the Kangia Icefjord were number two. But I think we can spare a little to contribute to the new Center, in her name of course, if it would help."

"That is beyond generous," Hendrik said in amazement. "Especially given all that's happened. Thank you, every bit helps. We'll do your wife's memory proud and of course, you all will be welcome anytime."

Katya fed the puppies and closed the gate. She then left to find her father and brother.

Hendrik informed them that their stay at the Arctic Palace was on him and then told them more about the plans for the new research and education center. Ezzy thought it seemed to take his mind off all the trouble his wife had caused.

"What are your plans for the rest of the day?" Hendrik asked.

"I'd like to take one more hike out to the icefjord to take some photos," Dr. Skylar replied. "I mean all this time and I hardly have any pictures." He turned to his kids. "If that's okay with you two?"

Ezzy tapped her head. "I've got plenty of pictures right here," she moaned. "And no phone. A whale ate mine."

"We'll get you a new one as soon as we get home, Ez. What about you, Luke? You up for a few more icebergs?"

"Sure Dad, as long as we observe them from land. No more on, in or under the ice for me."

Hendrik smiled weakly at the boy. "You could do the planet hike."

"What's that?"

"As we have more and more tourists coming, we've been trying to create new activities for them. Last year, we created a planet hike from the village out to the northwest shore of the icefjord. Along the hike are sculptures of the planets with information about each one and the solar system. It starts in town with the sun and ends out at the fjord at Pluto and is about three miles round trip. It's an easy hike and part of it's on a boardwalk."

Dr. Skylar turned to Ezzy and Luke. "What do you say, kids?"

"Sounds cool," Luke replied.

Ezzy looked at Luke and then her father. "You two are nuts, but I guess I can handle one more hike. After that, no more icebergs for a while, okay?"

*   *   *

That afternoon they took a shuttle from the hotel to the start of the planet walk. Beginning at the sun, they hiked to Mercury then Venus and on to Earth, Mars, Jupiter and Saturn. Luke was their official sign reader and ran ahead whenever they neared a new sculpture aka planet. Dr. Skylar happily played paparazzi, taking photos of Ezzy and Luke along the way. Ezzy was less enthused than her brother. She was still tired and missed her phone.

"We're almost to the edge of the icefjord," her father announced. "It's boardwalk the rest of the way and soon we'll get to see all the giant icebergs mashed together."

"Oh great," muttered Ezzy.

Dr. Skylar turned to his son. "What's the next planet?"

The boy looked at a map they'd picked up at the start of the trail and snickered.

"What?" his father asked.

"Uranus," Luke said giggling.

"We're going to *Ur-anus?*" Dr. Skylar said winking at Ezzy. "How far is it to *Ur-anus?*"

A hint of a smile appeared on her face.

Luke giggled some more and peered down at the boardwalk. "Look there's a long crack. We can just follow the crack to *Ur-anus.*" He burst into laughter.

Ezzy couldn't help herself. She laughed along with her brother and father.

The bad jokes about Uranus continued until they reached the planet and edge of the icefjord. Even after all they'd been through, Ezzy had to admit the jumble of icebergs at the mouth of the Kangia Icefjord was still one of the most amazing things she'd ever seen. She noticed a new pool of turquoise water shaped like an hourglass on one iceberg and an overhang on another that resembled a breaking wave. They heard a crack and watched as a large chunk broke off an iceberg, crashed into the water, and split into pieces, which were swept downstream with the current.

"Let me get one with you two in front of the icebergs," their father said. He adjusted the focus and snapped a photo. "That's gonna be a winner. And I know exactly who we should send it to."

"Who?" Luke asked.

"Our adventurous elderly friends and heroes from the Galápagos, Gracie and Phil Smith. Remember them? I forgot to tell you they texted and want to join us on our next trip—number three on mom's wonder list."

Luke and Ezzy stared at their father.

"You're gonna love it."

* * *

Note from the Author:
Real vs Made Up

A few years ago, while doing research for another book, I went to Ilulissat, Greenland. I spent hours hiking out to and around the Kangia Icefjord. It was one of the most amazing things I've ever witnessed and truly a wonder of nature. Teams of scientists from around the world also travel to Ilulissat to study the nearby glacier, floating ice shelf, and icefjord. They are investigating how climate change is impacting the area, how fast the ice is melting and how exactly it is happening. While I was in Ilulissat, I also went kayaking in a dry suit, took a boat ride up to the Equi Glacier to watch it calve, and greatly enjoyed wandering around the village. Much of what happens in the story is based on real science, but some is pure fiction. Once again, which do you think is real and which made-up? Answers follow.

The Sermaq Kujalleq or Jakobshavns Isbræ glacier is one of the fastest flowing rivers of ice in the world.

The iceberg that sank the Titanic was shed from the Kangia Icefjord.

Where the icebergs are big enough and flat, you can go hiking across them.

Due to an underwater ridge at the mouth of the fjord, a backup or traffic jam of icebergs occurs in the Kangia Icefjord.

Collapses at the ice shelf, which is hundreds of feet tall, create icebergs and even tsunamis.

Some of the icebergs look like they are bleeding brown blood.

Blue ice has no air in it.

The moulins or big holes in the glacier and ice shelf connect under the ice to form tunnels.

Scientists rappel into the moulins to deploy instruments under the ice.

Researchers have discovered that submarine melting is contributing to melting of the ice shelves and glaciers in Greenland.

Greenland dogs are the only type of dogs in Greenland.

Greenland dogs regularly howl from near and faraway.

During the summer months they put all-terrain wheels on the dog sleds for tourist rides.

A humpback whale surfaced right next to a boat, spouted, and showered a person aboard.

Humpback whales can be identified by the patterns on their tail flukes.

Humpbacks use bubble-nets to feed.

In bubble-net feeding, humpback whales have come up under boats and even capsized them.

Under the ice, there are giant lakes in big caverns.

Sometimes seawater glows in the dark.

Geothermal heat is a source of energy in Greenland.

Someone was caught trying to use geothermal heat to melt a glacier to get more freshwater.

You can hike from the village of Ilulissat out to the Kangia Icefjord to see icebergs.

Refrozen icebergs are freshwater.

The Sermaq Kujalleq or Jakobshavns Is-bræ glacier is one of the fastest flowing rivers of ice in the world.

Real. In the Summer of 2012, scientists measured the glacier moving at an amazing speed of 150 feet per day. Typically, the ice flows at a still quick 65 feet per day. It is one of the world's fastest flowing glaciers.

The iceberg that sank the Titanic was shed from the Kangia Icefjord.

Real. At least we think so. The glacier and ice shelf produce a lot of icebergs. The really big ones float north caught in ocean currents and pushed by the wind. They then head west toward Canada and south in another ocean current. These icebergs can last for years and have been sighted as far south as the same latitude as New Jersey.

Where the icebergs are big enough and flat, you can go hiking across them.

Made Up. It is dangerous to get too close to the icebergs or go out on them as they can collapse, roll over, or break apart.

Due to an underwater ridge at the mouth of the fjord, a backup or traffic jam of icebergs occurs in the Kangia Icefjord.

Real. It can take weeks or even months for the icebergs to melt enough to float off the ridge and out of the icefjord and into Disko Bay.

Collapses at the ice shelf, which is hundreds of feet tall, create icebergs and even tsunamis.

Real. Sometimes the ice breaks apart in small pieces, but sometimes enormous chunks fall off or collapse from the ice shelf, which creates giant icebergs and waves moving down through the fjord.

Some of the icebergs look like they are bleeding brown blood.

Real. Sediment gets trapped in the ice, making it look brown. The brown ice absorbs the sun's heat faster than the white ice and it melts quicker. Water running down the ice can look like brown blood with dirt and pebbles in it.

Blue ice has no air in it.

Real. White ice has air in it, but in blue ice the air has been squeezed out by the weight of the overlying ice or by refreezing.

The moulins or big holes in the glacier and ice shelf connect under the ice to form tunnels.

Made Up. They don't really form tunnels that you can kayak through, but it sure would be cool if they did and you could.

Scientists rappel into the moulins to deploy instruments under the ice.

Real. Some very brave scientists use ropes to go down into the moulins to place instruments in and under the ice. But it is dangerous, and they have to be very careful.

Researchers have discovered that submarine melting is contributing to melting of the ice shelves and glaciers in Greenland.

Real. Relatively warm (still cold) ocean water welling up into the fjords has been discovered in and around Greenland and Antarctica and is an important contributor to the melting of glaciers and ice shelves.

Greenland dogs are the only type of dogs in Greenland.

Real. Greenlanders do not allow any other type of dog in Greenland because they don't want them to intermix and breed, which could lead to the loss of the pure Greenland dog. These sled dogs are an important part of the history and culture in Greenland.

Greenland dogs regularly howl from near and far away.

Real. And it is a really eerie sound (check it out on the Internet by searching for Greenland dogs).

During the summer months they put all-terrain wheels on the dog sleds for tourist rides.

Made Up. But maybe they should.

A humpback whale surfaced right next to a boat, spouted, and showered a person aboard.

Real. It was not in Greenland, but I saw this happen to someone aboard a tall sailing ship in the Gulf of Maine (I was teaching oceanography out at sea).

Humpback whales can be identified by the patterns on their tail flukes.

Real. Each fluke has a unique black and white pattern. Scientists document these patterns and use them to identify and track individual whales.

Humpbacks use bubble-nets to feed.

Real. They work as a group to blow bubbles with their blowholes that rise to the surface like a net for small fish, plankton, and krill. Then the whales rise up underneath with their mouths open and take a big gulp full.

In bubble-net feeding, humpback whales have come up under boats and even capsized them.

Made Up. But they can come up very close by. In 2020, after this was written, a humpback whale feeding came up under a kayaker and tipped it over.

Under the ice, there are giant lakes in big caverns.

Real and Made Up. Real in that there are giant lakes under the ice in Greenland and Antarctica. But the big cavern as described in the book is made up.

Sometimes seawater glows in the dark.

Real. This is called bioluminescence. Many creatures in the ocean are able to produce light and they use it to lure in prey, scare predators, in communication, or as a decoy for escape. The type of bioluminescence described in the book is due to small one-celled organisms called dinoflagellates. They are like algæ. Water motion triggers their light production and it looks like sparkling in the water at night.

Geothermal heat is a source of energy in Greenland.

Real. They use heat from deep underground as part of their power supply.

Someone was caught trying to use geo-thermal heat to melt a glacier to get more freshwater.

Made Up. No one has been caught yet trying to melt a glacier or ice shelf for their own benefit.

You can hike from the village of Ilulissat out to the Kangia Icefjord to see icebergs.

So Real. If I remember correctly it takes less than thirty minutes to hike from the village out to the icefjord. There are trails, and in some places, boardwalks. And when you hike over the rocky ridges and see the icefjord for the first time it is mouth-open eyes-wide astonishing!

Refrozen icebergs are freshwater.

Real. I went kayaking near the icebergs in Disko Bay, and our guide picked up a transparent chunk of ice, chipped some off, and gave it to us to drink. It was delicious freshwater.

Also real are:

Humpback whales leap high out of the ocean or breach, but we don't know why exactly. It may be a way to communicate,

to remove parasites, or simply for fun.

The frozen ground is called permafrost and it is thawing in Greenland and around the Arctic. Due to permafrost thaw, roads in the Arctic become wavy, forests collapse, and the ground is turning to mush and mud.

In the movie *Chasing Ice*, the filmmakers caught the largest ever recorded collapse at the ice shelf upstream of the Kangia Icefjord (https://www.youtube.com/watch?v=oXe7T4SQNts).

There are reindeer, musk ox, seals, and fox in Greenland.

Climate Change

Climate change is real, human activities are the main cause, and it is impacting all of us, but it is having an especially big impact on places in the Arctic like Greenland. Each year, billions of tons of ice are melting in Greenland (and Antarctica). If the ice comes from land-based glaciers, the resulting meltwater is a significant contributor to sea level rise. Thawing of permafrost is also occurring and releasing more methane and carbon dioxide (greenhouse gases) into the atmosphere. Permafrost thaw also damages roads and can cause buildings to collapse. Having less ice in the winter is also changing the lives of people in the Arctic and the ecosystems they depend on. We created these problems and we can fix them. We all need to work together to reduce our emissions of carbon dioxide, conserve energy, eat less meat, plant more trees, reduce our food wastes, and do everything we can to help reduce climate change and protect the planet and our future.

Acknowledgments

The writing and publication of a book takes a team and I am grateful to mine. From the friends and family that provide continued encouragement to Penny Noyce and all the folks at Tumblehome that make the final product happen, my sincere thanks. To Linda, Kathy, and others, thank you for always being there, bringing me joy, and excellent advice along with moral support. A special thank you to Dave, not only for bringing so much love and laughter into my life, but also for one particularly hilarious hike along the planet walk in Anchorage, Alaska! A huge nod of gratitude to Christie Henry, formally with University Chicago Press, whose enthusiastic support of my popular science non-fiction efforts allowed me to travel to Ilulissat, Greenland. My experience there was unforgettable and inspirational, providing fantastic real-world tidbits to integrate into the story. Thank you to all the people I met in Greenland who were so kind, interesting, and made the experience all the better. Thanks to Tim (and Jackie) Dixon for suggesting Ilulissat and sharing his and his colleagues work in the area. Appreciation also goes to Penny Noyce for her excellent story advice and thoughtful editing, to hard working and responsive Yu-Yi, Natalie, and all the others at Tumblehome. Thanks to Tammy Yee for the wonderful cover. Much appreciation also to Debbi Stone (and Olivia) and the others at The Florida Aquarium for their relentless and energetic support of education and the first book in the series, *Escape Galápagos*. Thanks to Heather and Hallie for some terrific advice over lunch on some themes to include. To my precious test readers, Carlos, July, Hugo, Kathy, Susan, Cristina, Ronit and The Taylors, your input was invaluable and continues to amaze and inspire me—giant thank you and hugs. And finally, to my readers, you are why I write. Your notes, reviews, and tweets bring tears of joy and warmth to my heart. Keep reading, keep learning, and keep laughing.

About The Author

Dr. Ellen Prager is a marine scientist and author, widely recognized for her expertise and ability to make science entertaining and understandable for people of all ages. She currently works as a freelance writer, consultant, Chief Scientist for Storm Center Communications, and science advisor to Celebrity Cruises in the Galapagos Islands. She was previously the Chief Scientist for the Aquarius Reef Base program in Key Largo, Florida and the Assistant Dean at the University of Miami's Rosenstiel School of Marine and Atmospheric Science. Dr. Prager has built a national reputation as a scientist and spokesperson, serving as a consultant for the Disney movie *Moana* and appearing on The Today Show, Good Morning America, CBS Early Show, CNN, Fox News, The Weather Channel, and Discovery Channel. She is the author of numerous popular science books and the successful *Tristan Hunt and the Sea Guardians* series of middle-grade adventure novels.